LONG TRAIL TO NIRVANA

Bounty hunter Dean Kennedy returns to Dry Creek after another successful hunt, only to find that his wife Emily has struck up a friendship with outlaw Wolfe Lord. Kennedy reckons his problems are over when the sheriff runs Lord out of town, but then his wife and young son disappear. It takes him fifteen years to track Lord down, and the trail eventually leads him to the lawless town of Nirvana — where he makes some disturbing discoveries about the fates of those he has sought so long . . .

Books by Scott Connor
in the Linford Western Library:

AMBUSH IN DUST CREEK
SILVER GULCH FEUD
GOLDEN SUNDOWN
CLEARWATER JUSTICE
ESCAPE FROM FORT BENTON
RETURN TO BLACK ROCK
LAST STAGE TO LONESOME
McGUIRE, MANHUNTER
RAIDERS OF THE MISSION
SAN JUAN
COLTAINE'S REVENGE
STAND-OFF AT COPPER TOWN
SIEGE AT HOPE WELLS
THE SONS OF CASEY O'DONNELL
RIDE THE SAVAGE RIVER
HIGH NOON IN SNAKE RIDGE
THE LAND OF LOST DREAMS
THE HONOUR OF THE BADGE
SHOT TO HELL
RECKONING AT EL DORADO

SCOTT CONNOR

LONG TRAIL
TO NIRVANA

Complete and Unabridged

LINFORD
Leicester

First published in Great Britain in 2016 by
Robert Hale
an imprint of The Crowood Press
Wiltshire

First Linford Edition
published 2019
by arrangement with
The Crowood Press
Wiltshire

A catalogue record for this book is available
from the British Library.

ISBN 978–1–4448–4074–2

Published by
F. A. Thorpe (Publishing)
Anstey, Leicestershire

Set by Words & Graphics Ltd.
Anstey, Leicestershire
Printed and bound in Great Britain by
T. J. International Ltd., Padstow, Cornwall

This book is printed on acid-free paper

1

The men sitting around the fire were settling down for the night, so Dean Kennedy shuffled closer to the edge of the rise.

He had been tracking Verne Allen and his band of outlaws for a week and now for the first time he had them in his sights. They had made their camp in an area where three massive boulders abutted each other to create a protected location.

The boulders were too large for anyone to scale and the camp could be entered from only one direction. So for the last two hours a guard, Jacques, had been standing beyond the opening to the campsite, his presence being enough to ensure the outlaws wouldn't suffer any surprises.

Last month Dean had recruited one of Verne's gang — while holding a gun to his head — to help him bring down Verne. So far this man, Brewster Kelly, had complied with Dean's instructions by helping him plan this raid and then leaving clues about Verne's movements for him to follow.

If they were successful, Brewster's reward would be his freedom. Dean's reward would be the bounty on Verne's head and, hopefully, information about an even bigger prize. But to succeed Dean had to hope Brewster would complete his side of the bargain.

When weak light from the low crescent moon had replaced the twilight redness lighting the western horizon Brewster moved away from the fire to speak to Jacques. This was the signal to Dean that he should make his move.

Dean slipped back from the edge of the rise and made his way down to ground level, using the path he'd picked out earlier. This route let him come out at the side of the boulder to the right of the entrance, where he gathered his breath and listened.

As he heard nothing to suggest the outlaws had heard him approaching he edged forward to look along the front of the boulder. All was still, while Brewster and Jacques were sitting on a rock around twenty yards from the entrance.

Brewster was deep in conversation with Jacques; both men were peering at the plains ahead, so Dean made his stealthy way along the front of the boulder. He walked sideways with his back to the rock until he reached the entrance to the camp, where he again stopped to listen.

The three outlaws were now bustling about. Verne was talking to the other two men, Eddie and Yale, his voice low and commanding, suggesting he was delivering orders. Dean had hoped to burst into the camp while the men were resting up, but the distraction offered by their listening to Verne would work just as well, so he nudged his head forward to peer into the camp.

The situation was as he'd imagined it. Verne was thirty paces away. He was standing side-on to him and gesturing at Yale and Eddie, who were sitting back against the boulder on Dean's side of the camp.

As their attention was on Verne and the light from the guarded campfire didn't extend to the entrance, Dean drew his gun. Then, with it held down, he moved on into the camp.

The weak moonlight played across the first ten yards of the entrance, but on Dean's side the shadows were deep. Feeling confident that he wouldn't be seen until he reached the circle of firelight around the campfire, Dean walked quietly with his back to the rock.

He managed ten short paces without the outlaws showing any sign that they were aware he was there, but then his foot scraped over a stone. The noise silenced Verne and he turned smartly; then to Dean's relief he looked out through the entrance.

'Did you hear that?' he asked.

'That was probably Jacques and

Brewster,' Yale said unconcernedly.

'It probably was, but I can't see them from here. Go and check out what they're doing.'

Yale grumbled but Eddie slapped him on the shoulder.

'The quicker you go,' he said, 'the quicker we can all get some sleep.'

Yale nodded and, still muttering to himself, he got up and made his way towards the entrance. He stretched his neck as he sought an early sighting of the guards, and that kept his gaze away from Dean.

Dean breathed shallowly while keeping an eye on all three visible outlaws. He didn't reckon that his luck in avoiding being seen would hold out for much longer and, sure enough, when Yale had covered half the distance to the entrance he flinched and then looked directly at Dean.

Yale stopped and cocked his head to one side, suggesting he was unsure whether he could see someone lurking in the darkness, but his action made

Verne edge his hand towards his holster while Eddie jumped to his feet.

Dean jerked up his gun arm. He sighted Yale and blasted off a shot that caught him low in the chest. Yale doubled over.

A second shot, higher on the chest, made him drop down on his knees. Even as Yale was keeling over on to his front, Dean abandoned all caution and moved forward purposefully.

Verne took flight across the camp while Eddie swung up his gun to sight Dean. Before Dean could aim at him, Eddie blasted a shot that sliced into the rock several feet in front of Dean's right arm. Then he followed through with three rapid shots that splayed lead to Dean's left.

As Eddie clearly hadn't worked out his exact location, Dean took his time in aiming. His first shot slammed into his target's forehead, cracking his head back before he keeled over on to his back. Then he swung his arm to the side to pick out the outlaw leader.

Verne was running away from him but he must have been aware of the danger he was in, as he dived to the ground, rolled, and then sought a hiding-place on the other side of the camp. Dean hurried Verne on his way with a gunshot that sliced into the ground behind him, but then Verne scrambled into a niche in the boulder.

Dean slapped the rock in irritation, then moved on quickly. He ran three paces to draw level with Yale's body, but Verne lunged forward into view with his gun already raised.

Verne tore out two quick shots, picking him out so well that Dean was sure he heard a slug whistle by inches from his right ear, while the other gunshot made his hat kick as it caught it a glancing blow.

Before Dean could return fire Verne darted back out of sight. So, taking a sudden decision Dean scurried across the camp, trying to ensure that he was in an unexpected position when Verne next risked emerging.

He jumped over Yale's body, then thrust his head down as he moved on quickly. Keeping his gun trained on the recess where Verne was hiding, he scampered to the other side without Verne showing himself again.

He glanced at the entrance, but neither Brewster nor Jacques was visible. Brewster's task was to overcome Jacques and Dean hoped the lack of noise coming from that direction meant he had already done that.

Then, as he had done on the other side of the camp, Dean moved on walking sideways with his back to the boulder. He expected Verne to act quickly, but when he'd moved to within three paces of the niche without Verne making his next move, he saw the reason for his failure to appear.

From the other side of the camp the recess had looked to be only a few feet deep, but now that he was closer he could see that the boulder had a deep crack, its depths hidden in dark shadows where the firelight didn't reach and which could stretch back for some distance.

Wasting no time, he reloaded. Then he ducked down and hurried into the niche keeping his head held low.

The moment he faced the dark unknown he went down on one knee and splayed gunfire in an arc. He aimed low, hoping that he would only wound Verne, so that he could capture him alive.

Slugs whined and echoed as they ricocheted and Dean got the impression that his shots all hit rock close by. As he didn't reckon he'd caught Verne with a lucky shot, he threw himself down on his side.

He aimed towards the centre of the darkness as he waited for a sign of where Verne had gone to ground. Long moments passed in silence before he detected movement.

It was only a shifting in the level of darkness that could have been a trick of the poor light, and strangely it came from around eight feet above him.

He aimed at that spot, but as he'd already fired four times he held his fire. Then he wished he'd trusted his instincts when Verne came hurtling down at him.

He just had time to work out that Verne must have clambered up on to a ledge, from which he was now leaping down before his opponent slammed down on him.

All the air blasted out of Dean's chest in a rush and Verne added to his problems when he grabbed his shoulders and slammed his head back against the rocky ground. Then he batted Dean's right hand down on the ground, knocking his six-shooter from his grasp.

Verne settled his weight down on him with a knee on either side of his hips, one arm pinning his chest down, and a gun aimed at his head. He grinned, his teeth bright in the poor light.

'Before you die, tell me who you are,' he demanded.

Dean squirmed and succeeded in

moving his right arm a few inches, but he couldn't shift Verne's body.

'I'm Dean Kennedy, bounty hunter.' Dean smiled. 'I'm the best there is.'

Verne looked him over and snorted in derision.

'To even think you could take me on, you'd have to be the best, but you failed.'

Dean shrugged, the action letting him move his right arm again until his fingers touched the holster of the second gun he kept hidden in his inside pocket.

'You're nothing. I only want you because of someone you once associated with, Wolfe Lord.'

'I've never heard of him.'

Verne tensed, suggesting he wouldn't say anything more and that he was preparing to shoot. So Dean jerked his right hand round and in a deft movement he fired up into Verne's lower chest.

Verne lurched forward as Dean fired a second time. Then Dean twisted away.

Verne didn't return fire, but Dean still squirmed out from under Verne's body and leapt to his feet. He trained the gun on his opponent and loomed over him.

'Last chance to talk,' he said. 'Tell me where and when you last saw Wolfe and I'll get you to help.'

'Never met this Wolfe,' Verne murmured. Then with a rattling croak he tensed and stilled.

Dean nudged him in the side and urged him to speak, but Verne didn't react. Dean grunted in irritation as yet another tenuous lead amounted to nothing.

Then he slipped his second gun away and holstered his fallen six-shooter. Walking backwards, he dragged Verne out into the stronger light.

He had covered half the distance to the fire when shuffling sounded behind him. He turned to find that Brewster had arrived.

Brewster was sporting a lively grin and he had his gun drawn and aimed at

Verne. Dean released Verne's body and straightened up.

'I assume you dealt with Jacques,' he said.

Brewster frowned. 'When the shooting started Jacques ran for his life. I followed him, but he got away in the dark.'

'Getting Jacques was the only task you had to do, and you failed. If I hadn't been careful Verne could have blasted me to hell.'

'He could have, but that'd have just meant there was more bounty for me.'

Dean narrowed his eyes. 'I told you when I recruited you that you're not getting none of the bounty out of this.'

Brewster glanced at his gun, then raised it to aim at Dean's chest.

'I remember what you said.' Brewster chuckled. 'But I reckon now might be the time for us to discuss our partnership again.'

2

Dean spread his hands, but he kept his right hand close to his holster.

'We're not discussing nothing because we're not partners,' he said. 'Our deal was that you'd lead me to Verne Allen and in return I wouldn't turn you in for the bounty on your head.'

Brewster frowned. 'Except while you've been safely following the clues I left for you, I've been taking all the risks. If Verne had worked out that I was double-crossing him, I'd be dead and you wouldn't have beaten him.'

Dean nodded and took a pace towards Brewster.

'I guess you're right. So what have you got in mind?'

'I'm not a greedy man. I reckon half the bounty should be enough to satisfy me.'

Dean kept moving forward. 'The

bounty on Verne is five hundred dollars. Two-fifty is a lot of money for a man who only did what I told him to do.'

'Except I need that money to get far away from here and lie low, and half the bounty isn't that much to ask for when I have a gun on you.' Brewster chuckled. 'I believe you said something similar when you persuaded me to help you find Verne.'

Dean took two more paces which brought him standing in front of Brewster. He rubbed his jaw, half-turning to consider the bodies lying around the camp.

When he saw that Brewster was following his gaze Dean swung back and thudded a swinging punch into Brewster's jaw. The blow lifted Brester's feet off the ground before he slammed down on his back.

In a moment Dean was on him, sweeping away his gun and then grabbing his collar to raise his head. Brewster's eyes started to close, so Dean slapped his face back and forth until Brewster's eyes focused on him.

In a moment Dean was on him, sweeping away his gun and then grabbing his collar to raise his head. Brewster's eyes started to close, so Dean slapped his face back and forth until Brewster's eyes focused on him.

Dean waited until Brewster groaned, then he winked.

'In that case you've got yourself a deal,' he said.

★ ★ ★

Five days after leaving Verne's camp Dean rode into Dry Creek. He had failed to find Jacques, the outlaw who had escaped, and the bodies of the three dead outlaws were strapped down over their horses, trailing behind Brewster.

Dean had given Brewster the duty of looking after them, figuring that the responsibility would reduce the chances of the wanted man confronting him again. They hadn't discussed the allocation of the bounty after the altercation at the camp, but Dean reckoned that Brewster wouldn't expect him to accept his opening demand: that they split the bounty equally.

Dean rode on until he was one building away from the law office. Then he stopped and waited for Brewster to join him.

'This is where we part company,' he said.

'I'm going nowhere until you've been in there and collected the bounty,' Brewster said cautiously.

'Except that, as you want to avoid meeting the law, you should leave now.' Dean withdrew a small wad of bills from his pocket. 'There's around twenty-five dollars here. That should be enough for you to lie low for a while.'

Brewster shook his head. 'I want two hundred and fifty, not twenty-five.'

'You're getting twenty-five plus your freedom, and for a man who isn't no use to me no more, that's more generous than I need to be.'

Brewster frowned. 'I reckon I can still be useful to you. We made a good team. I worked on the inside gaining Verne's trust and you worked on the outside waiting for my signal to blast him to hell. So what about a new partnership?'

'We can't form a new partnership, because we were never partners.'

'Yeah, but I've been thinking and I reckon I could get close to other outlaws. Verne once rode with Sebastian Crow and he was talking about joining him for a big raid Sebastian's planning. The last I heard the bounty on him was four thousand dollars.'

'I'm not interested in Sebastian or in spending more time with you.' Dean smiled. 'Unless you can help me fill in some missing details about Verne, such as his association with Wolfe Lord.'

Brewster looked aloft as he gave the matter serious consideration. Then he shook his head.

'I've never met or heard of that man and Verne never mentioned him.'

'Then you're no use to me no more.'

Dean raised the money for emphasis, and with a snarl Brewster reached over and snatched it from his hand.

Brewster licked his lips, seemingly preparing to deliver a threat, but the bodies had now gathered attention and people were gravitating across the main drag. So he limited himself to glaring at Dean before he moved his horse on.

Brewster galloped past the law office looking as if he'd hurry out of town, but the lure of the saloon on the edge of town made him draw his horse to a halt. Dean reckoned he wasn't taking too big a risk of being recognized as, despite Brewster's concern, his crimes hadn't gathered him that much notoriety.

Dean dismounted and before he reached the law office Sheriff Quigley emerged. He regarded Dean's haul with approval, then he dispatched a deputy to deal with the bodies while he and Dean headed inside.

'You did well to bring in Verne,' Quigley said. 'But I guess that's why you had help this time.'

'Sure,' Dean said. He walked across to examine the display of Wanted posters to avoid talking about Brewster in case it gave him problems later.

'Did Verne get you any closer to Wolfe Lord?'

'No. Just before he breathed his last Verne claimed that he'd never met him, and I reckon he told the truth. The information I'd got that they once knew each other was vague and the informer was even more unreliable.' He turned back to the Wanted posters.

The most prominent of them drew his attention first. Quigley noticed his interest and came over to stand at his shoulder.

'Sebastian Crow is getting every bounty hunter interested. His bounty's gone up by another thousand since the last time you were here.'

Brewster had claimed that Verne once rode with Sebastian, but Dean judged that link back to Wolfe to be so tenuous and the risks involved in bringing

Sebastian to justice so great that it wasn't worth considering. So he examined the details of the men with smaller bounties on their heads.

'Five thousand dollars is a lot of money,' he said. 'Then again, Sebastian Crow is a lot of trouble.'

'I understand. I should have Verne's bounty for you tomorrow morning once I've confirmed the details.' Quigley then lowered his voice. 'But don't leave town too quickly. You need to see someone.'

Dean noted Quigley's sombre tone and that made him straighten up.

'Who?'

'Harwood Manning fell ill last month and he's been fading away quickly. Apparently he'll be lucky to see out the week.'

Dean turned. 'I vowed never to talk to Harwood again and I doubt he'd want to make his peace with me before the end.'

'I doubt that, too. On the other hand, if he doesn't talk to you now, he never will.'

Dean conceded Quigley's point with a stern nod and then headed to the door. Outside he looked down the main drag at Harwood's hotel and considered what he could say to make him talk.

He doubted that anything he might say would persuade Harwood to break his silence, so with a heavy heart he moved on. When he reached the saloon opposite the hotel he saw through the window that Brewster was at the bar and eyeing a poker game with interest.

Once upon a time, many years ago, he had often frequented that saloon and now the sight of it made him smile. In a slightly more contented frame of mind he headed to the hotel.

Harwood's son, Meldrick, was in the reception room; he sighed when he saw Dean.

'I'm certain my father wouldn't want to see you at a time like this,' he said. Then he offered Dean a sympathetic frown. 'On the other hand, he doesn't know you're in town, so he hasn't told me that he doesn't want to see you.'

'I'm obliged for your understanding,' Dean said. 'And I'm genuinely sorry to hear the news about his illness. Once we were friends and if there was anything I could do to put right what happened between us, I would.'

'I know that, but there's only one person who can change things.' Meldrick shrugged, acknowledging that he doubted his father would soften his stance, then he beckoned for Dean to follow him.

He led him into a back room where, despite the grave warnings Dean had received about Harwood's poor health, the old man was sitting up in bed. The moment Harwood saw Dean he snapped his arm up and pointed at the door.

'Are you trying to kill me off by bringing that man in here, boy?' he demanded, his voice shaking with barely suppressed anger. 'Get him out of my sight.'

'I reckon Meldrick thought that seeing me would liven you up,' Dean said. 'It seems to have worked.'

These were the first words he'd spoken to Harwood in twelve years. On hearing them Harwood glared at Meldrick, seemingly hoping that his son would comply with his demand so that he wouldn't have to deal with Dean. When Meldrick sat on a chair by the door, Harwood turned his his gaze upon Dean.

'I've still got nothing to say to you, Dean,' he said. 'So you've wasted a journey.'

'I'm in town because I'd completed another successful bounty hunt. I'm now looking for my next quarry and I thought you might like to help me.'

Harwood folded his arms. 'I don't.'

'If you won't talk to me about Wolfe Lord, is there anything you want to tell me about Emily?'

Harwood shook his head. 'If you figured that you could bully a dying man into talking about her, you thought wrong. Go away.'

Harwood snarled his last comment,

which induced a bout of coughing that made him lean forward, his face reddening by the moment.

Meldrick hurried across the room and helped him sit up straight. By degrees Harwood's coughing spluttered to an end, after which his son helped him lie on his back.

Now that Harwood really was looking like the ill man Dean had expected to see, Meldrick glanced at the door. Dean shook his head and moved around the other side of the bed, opposite Meldrick.

'I tried to be nice about this,' he muttered to Harwood, 'but you wouldn't listen, so now I'll have to find another way to get you to talk. I hope you're not strong enough to resist me.'

'That's enough,' Meldrick said, hurrying round the bed. 'I let you in here to talk to my father, not to threaten him.'

Dean ignored him and glared down at Harwood, who struggled to return his gaze. When Meldrick reached Dean he slapped a hand on his shoulder, but Dean shrugged him off.

Meldrick then moved to grab his arm, but Dean evaded his lunge and with a swipe of his arm he knocked him aside. Meldrick fell towards the bed and in seeking to avoid landing on his father he twisted and hit the corner of the bed. He went sprawling on the floor.

'Your son won't save you from what I could do to you, so talk, Harwood,' Dean growled, looming over the dying man.

Harwood tried to raise his head to see Meldrick, but he didn't have the strength to move. He could only look up at Dean with frightened eyes, opening and closing his mouth soundlessly. Then a determined gleam appeared in his eyes and he chuckled.

'Do you really want me to tell you the last thing Emily said to me?' he said, his voice now stronger than it had been.

'Sure,' Dean replied as Meldrick

clambered back to his feet and stood beside him.

'She told me that if you ever forced me to tell you about her, I should tell you to go to hell.'

Harwood cackled, but that induced another round of coughing. Dean waited until he'd silenced and then tipped his hat.

'I'm obliged you've told me that,' he said with a wide smile that he wasn't feigning. 'You see, I've always assumed she was dead, but if she told you that before she disappeared, that means Wolfe didn't kill her.'

Harwood's eyes opened wide, acknowledging that he'd made a mistake and revealed something he never had done before.

Meldrick grabbed Dean's arm but this time Dean didn't fight him, figuring that he'd got everything he ever would out of Harwood. He let Meldrick have the pleasure of escorting him out of the room and then across the reception area to the outside door.

'Don't ever come back here again,' Meldrick said when he released his arm.

As Meldrick marched away, Dean stood outside the hotel and thought about heading to the saloon and drinking with Brewster. Then he dismissed that notion with a shake of his head and turned to seek out another saloon. But after two paces he came to a halt.

Brewster was leaning against the corner of the hotel and he was watching him from under a lowered hat, a smile on his face.

'I've been asking in the saloon about you,' he said with a smirk. 'I heard some mighty interesting things.'

'If you're still hoping to get your hands on a share of Verne's bounty, you wasted your time.'

'I'm not interested in that bounty. I'm interested in your next one and this time, before we start hunting, I reckon we should agree a partnership based on trust and mutual understanding.'

Dean gave Brewster a long look, then he snorted a laugh.

'I told you that I'm not interested in tracking down Sebastian Crow, or anyone else where I need your help to find them.'

'Except there is one man who you'll accept my help to find.' Brewster licked his lips. 'I now know where you can find Wolfe Lord.'

Dean flinched, unable to hide his surprise.

'You just got my attention,' he said.

3

'So why do you want to find Wolfe?' Brewster asked, peering at Dean through the campfire flames.

Dean had been expecting this question all day, but since they'd left Dry Creek this morning they had ridden in silence. They had followed Brewster's instructions to head east towards the town of Hawkeye, and even when they'd made camp for the night they had been quiet until an hour after sundown.

'I'm a bounty hunter,' Dean said with a shrug.

'I've not heard anyone even mention that there's a bounty on Wolfe, and yet I was told you've been looking for him for the last fifteen years.'

'So you didn't lie when you said you'd been asking about me in the saloon.' Dean sighed. 'In which case you must know the rest.'

'I heard several versions from people who weren't even in town fifteen years ago, so as we'll be together for a while longer, I'd like to hear the truth.'

Dean leaned forward to pick up a stick. He poked the fire and then settled back, patting the end of the stick on the ground.

'Fifteen years ago I returned to town after another hunt to find that Wolfe Lord had settled down in Harwood Manning's hotel. Wolfe drank, fought, gambled, and I wouldn't have bothered even speaking with him except somehow he'd struck up a friendship with my wife Emily.'

Brewster chuckled. 'The people I talked with reckoned they were more than just friends.'

'I don't care what other people think,' Dean snapped. 'Emily was a fine woman and Wolfe was a waste of skin.'

'Sometimes men like that are appealing to certain women.' Brewster licked his lips. 'I've certainly delighted my share of womenfolk.'

Dean whipped up his hand to point the stick at Brewster.

'Never say anything like that about her again.' Dean waited, but Brewster didn't reply, so he lowered the stick. 'Anyway, Wolfe got into trouble so often that Sheriff Quigley told him to leave town by sundown, and he did.'

'And Emily left with him?'

'I don't know. That's where my knowledge of events ends. All I know for certain is that she went to the hotel before Wolfe left and Harwood Manning spoke with her, but she never came back to me.'

Brewster pondered on Dean's words; when he spoke his tone was low and more compassionate than it had been before.

'I know you don't want me commenting on what happened, but it sounds to me like she wasn't happy that Wolfe was being run out of town. After a cosy chat in the hotel, they decided to leave together.'

Dean sighed. 'My assumption at the time was that Wolfe had kidnapped and then killed her. Sheriff Quigley agreed with me, but neither of us could find her or Wolfe, and Harwood wouldn't talk about what had happened in his hotel.'

'He'd been paid to keep his silence?'

'That's what I figured, but after a few weeks with no new information the investigation died out. Despite that, I resolved never to rest until I found Emily, or found Wolfe and learned the truth about what happened to her. I searched for a year until I'd used up every scrap of a lead that I had. Then I returned to searching for minor outlaws like you.'

'My loss,' Brewster murmured.

'As the years went by Wolfe occasionally resurfaced, but I never got close to him. Then a few years ago the trail went completely cold and I was left searching for men who might once have met him, such as Verne Allen.'

Brewster raised a surprised eyebrow.

'Fifteen years is a long time to search for a woman and the man who stole her away from you.'

'Until I spoke with Harwood yesterday I'd always assumed she'd been killed, and I guess that despite him admitting she didn't want me, I'd still like to know for sure if she's alive.'

'So why keep looking?'

Dean poked at the fire again while he pondered on whether he wanted to reveal the rest. As he could think of no reason why he shouldn't, he looked up at Brewster.

'Because it's not just about her. We had a five-year-old son, Clement, and he disappeared with her.'

'Ah,' Brewster said, lowering his head.

'So I had to keep looking because if they hadn't been killed, that meant she didn't want me, but my son didn't get a say about whether he needed his father.'

Dean hurled the stick on the fire. Then he raised an eyebrow, giving

Brewster the opportunity to explain where he was taking him.

'As you know, I've seen some trouble and I've associated with people I shouldn't have.'

Dean snorted a laugh. 'Your Wanted poster lists so many crimes, it almost needs a second page.'

Brewster laughed. 'Most are petty crimes, some got added because I have a reputation, and as for the rest, I merely associated with men who did bad things.'

'Does that include Wolfe?'

'Yeah. I was given a description of him in Dry Creek and I was with Verne when he met a man who matched that description. That man was living quietly under the name of Finlay Jackson in Hawkeye.'

Dean winced. He had covered vast distances in his search, but if Brewster was right, Wolfe had once been only a week's ride away from Dry Creek.

'Which probably explains why the trail died out. Did you see a woman with him, or a young man?'

'No, but then again I wasn't looking. Verne and me played poker with him and I won, but Finlay refused to pay up. We argued, but he warned me off by convincing me that he had a ruthless past. I decided not to press the matter.'

'I feel real sorry for you. How long ago was that?'

'Six months.' Brewster smiled. 'And the thing is, I gather that this Finlay Jackson had been living in a hotel there for a while.'

Dean nodded in agreement. 'It sounds as if that's a habit of his, in which case your lead could be a good one.'

'Good enough for half the bounty?'

Dean rubbed his chin, as if thinking. In truth he wanted to find Wolfe only because of what he knew about the whereabouts of Emily and Clement.

There had never been any proof that Wolfe had harmed them and his criminal activities hadn't been serious enough to warrant a bounty on his head, but he figured Brewster didn't need to know that.

'If you lead me to Wolfe, it's a deal,' he said.

★ ★ ★

A week after leaving Dry Creek Dean and Brewster rode into Hawkeye.

Brewster pointed out the hotel where Wolfe had been staying when they'd played poker. Then, with Brewster advising caution, they rode around the outskirts of town.

Dean tried to foster an optimistic feeling that his first lead in years might lead him to Wolfe, but after so many disappointments and with his hopes relying on Brewster, he eyed the back of the hotel with scepticism. So when Brewster kept riding past the building, he didn't complain.

Dean noted that the hotel looked like the kind of run-down establishment that Wolfe might have made his base. Then he followed Brewster as he rode past the edge of town and up a rise.

Brewster stopped just below the crest of the rise and turned to face the town. Dean followed his lead in swinging round to peer down at the hotel.

'As we passed I saw the sign on the side of the hotel,' Brewster said. 'It's still owned by Siegfried Forester, so he should be able to help you.'

'If Wolfe is still in one of his rooms, Siegfried won't need to answer any questions,' Dean said.

Brewster frowned and jumped down from his horse. Then he led it over the rise.

Dean followed him and found that he was heading to a fenced-in cemetery. Brewster tethered his horse to a post; then, without looking at Dean, he clambered over the fence.

Dean noted that Brewster avoided catching his eye, but he also figured that Brewster would only explain what was on his mind in his own time, so he too climbed into the cemetery. He caught up with Brewster when he stopped beside a grave.

A small cross bore only the initials FJ, which at first meant nothing to him. Then he flinched and swirled round to face Brewster, who nodded.

'A man who called himself Finlay Jackson is buried here,' Brewster said, 'although you knew him as Wolfe Lord.'

'Wolfe is dead?' Dean murmured, aghast at this unwelcome turn of events.

'He sure is, and that means this will be the easiest bounty we'll ever earn.'

Brewster laughed and rubbed his hands, but Dean hunched his shoulders. Then he walked around the grave and kicked the cross over.

4

'How did you know Wolfe was dead and buried up here?' he asked, glaring down at the cross.

'After we'd played poker Verne wasn't as forgiving as I was,' Brewster said with a grin. 'He went back to town and shot him up.'

Dean picked up the cross and dashed it down on the ground, making the two pieces of wood break apart. He hurled them to either side and then swirled round to face Brewster.

'Then that was a fitting end for him, but you heard my story. I wanted Wolfe in order to find out what had happened to my wife and son, not to bring him in for the bounty.'

Brewster shrugged, appearing unmoved by his anger.

'When you told me your heart-rending tale Wolfe was already dead,

and people here will remember him.'
Brewster kicked at the mound of dirt.
'Even better, to claim the bounty on
him all we need is a strong stomach and
a spade.'

A flurry of anger made Dean's blood
race. If he'd had a spade with him he'd
have repaid Brewster's callous attitude
by burying it in his skull.

As it was, he contented himself with
pacing up to Brewster and grabbing his
collar.

'You knew how badly I'd take this,'
he grunted, dragging him up close. 'Yet
you let me think I'd find Wolfe alive
here.'

'You let me think you'd share the
bounty on Verne Allen, except you
didn't.' Brewster smirked. 'Now we're
even.'

Dean tightened his grip and bunched
a fist, but when Brewster regarded him
without concern he found that he felt
more tired than angry.

He hurled Brewster aside, making
him go to his knees. Then he flopped

down to sit on the end of the mound.

For several minutes he hunched forward and contemplated his hands. Then the thought hit him that even if Brewster reckoned he'd repaid him, his unwelcome associate had yet to find out that he'd gain nothing from digging up Wolfe's body.

With a sigh he forced himself to stop feeling dejected by this turn of events. He slapped his legs and stood up.

'I guess we are even now,' he said, pointing at the mound. 'I'll find out what Siegfried Forester knows about Wolfe while you find a spade.'

'I was afraid you'd say that.' Brewster sighed. 'Find out what you can and we'll meet up back here at sundown.'

'I don't reckon so. If you dig up Wolfe, you can have him.'

'But what about our partnership?'

'We're not partners.'

'That's as maybe, but I can't go into a law office. I need you to claim the bounty.'

Dean shrugged and without further

comment he moved off. Brewster shouted at him to come back, but Dean ignored him. He left the cemetery and rode into town on his own.

The short journey helped to calm him down and remove some of his irritation with Brewster as he accepted that, despite his dishonesty, the man had helped his quest.

At the hotel he dismounted and went straight in. He rang the bell on the reception desk several times before the owner sloped in.

'I'm looking for information on one of your regular customers, Finlay Jackson,' Dean said.

Siegfried narrowed his eyes and busied himself with moving the reception book a few inches to one side, his behaviour suggesting that Dean wasn't the first person to enquire about him.

'Finlay died six months ago,' Siegfried said. He set his hands on his hips. 'He paid his bills, and that's all I ask from a customer.'

'I'm sure he was good company.'

Dean leaned over the desk. 'But did he have anyone interesting with him, such as a woman?'

'Plenty of women visited him. I can't remember all their names.'

'I'm interested in one in particular. She might have arrived with him.'

Siegfried shook his head. 'He arrived on his own and then he kept his head down.'

'Did he ever talk about his reason for coming here, or what he was doing before?'

'You're asking an awful lot of questions about a dead man.' Siegfried gestured to one side. 'Finlay is buried up there and I reckon you should let him lie in peace.'

'Perhaps I will let *Finlay* lie in peace.'

Siegfried winced, acknowledging that he'd heard Dean's emphasis and that he knew its significance.

'You do that.' Siegfried turned and walked away.

'I'll be asking around town about him,' Dean called after him. 'I'll be sure to come back later and tell you what I've learned.'

Siegfried stopped for a moment, then walked on without responding further. So Dean went outside and headed to the nearest saloon.

He quizzed the bartender in a cautious manner about whether Sieg- fried's hotel was a decent place to rest up for a long stay. Without too much prompting his questions encouraged the bartender to talk about the only other person he could remember staying there for a long period of time.

He talked about Finlay arriving in town alone and living quietly until his demise. The description he provided of Finlay's appearance matched Dean's memories of Wolfe Lord, even if the details of his behaviour during his time here didn't match the way he'd behaved when Dean had known him.

Dean moved on, but as he worked his way around town he didn't add much to what he'd learnt already. Since Wolfe had apparently kept a low profile few people could even remember him, so Dean had to be increasingly direct in his attempts to gather information.

Before long word got around that someone was asking about a former townsman as well as about movements at Siegfried's hotel; this led to people refusing to talk to him.

By sundown the only thing Dean had confirmed was that Emily hadn't been with Wolfe. He settled down by the window in the saloon opposite the hotel, drinking and brooding about what he should do next.

He had watched the cemetery until the light level dropped, but he hadn't seen Brewster. He figured that the only option left open to him was that now he'd discovered Wolfe's final resting place, he needed to find out where he had been before he came here.

That wouldn't be an easy task, but Dean resolved not to move on until he got more answers and the best place to stay while he did that was Siegfried's hotel. With that resolution he left the saloon and headed across the main drag.

This time when he rang the bell Siegfried didn't appear, so he banged a fist on the desk. Still he failed to get a response. He figured Siegfried had probably seen him coming and had gone into hiding, so he looked in the back room.

Siegfried wasn't there so Dean returned to the desk. He opened the reception book and riffled through the pages until he found an entry from six months back.

Finlay Jackson was marked as being in residence in room seven. This room was currently unoccupied, as was the rest of the hotel, so Dean reckoned that this was a good room for him to take.

He searched for a key, but curiously it wasn't on the board upon which hung the other unused keys. With a shrug he headed to the stairs.

When he reached the corridor at the top of the stairs he could see that a door at the end of the corridor was open; counting along he calculated that this was room seven.

Feeling even more curious he walked on cautiously. After a few paces he heard people talking inside. He stopped to listen and although he couldn't hear what they were saying he recognized one voice as Siegfried's, the other as Brewster's.

Brewster was talking loudly, while Siegfried sounded defensive. Dean assumed that Brewster was doing what Dean had tried to do in seeking to get information, so he stopped being stealthy and moved on.

A slap sounded in the room, followed by a thud as, clearly, an altercation got under way. Then a gunshot blasted, the sound echoing down the corridor.

Dean stopped two doors away from the room and pressed himself to the wall. He drew his gun and levelled it on the door, but long moments passed without anyone emerging.

Then shuffling and creaking sounded in the room, suggesting that furniture was being moved. He walked quietly on to the doorway until Brewster became visible.

He was on his knees and rooting around behind a cabinet. Dean stepped into the doorway and winced when he saw that Siegfried was lying face down on the bed with blood seeping out from under his chest.

Dean raised his gun to aim at Brewster's back.

'What in tarnation are you doing?' he demanded.

Brewster flinched, then straightened up.

'I'm helping us out,' he said, and resumed feeling around behind the cabinet.

Dean side-stepped to the bed and nudged Siegfried in the side, but that made him slip off the bed taking the covers with him. When he flopped down lifelessly on the floor, Dean moved to stand over Brewster.

'How does killing a man who might know something about Wolfe help us?'

Brewster raised his head, smiled at him, then withdrew his arm from behind the cabinet. Clutched in his right hand was a bulging bag which, from the gleam in Brewster's eyes, presumably contained money.

'Because if you're not prepared to hand in Wolfe's body, this will provide some compensation.'

'Are you saying that's Wolfe's stash from his life of crime?'

'I'd worked out he must have hidden his money somewhere. Apparently, Siegfried's been spending it for the last six months, but there's still plenty left.'

'That money will have been stolen, so you can't claim it.'

'If you're not going to prove that the man who called himself Finlay Jackson is really Wolfe Lord, that means nobody can claim this money is Wolfe's.'

Dean couldn't think of an argument against this logic. He moved to the window. As he expected, the sound of gunfire had drawn people out on to the main drag.

50

A group had formed and half of them were peering at the hotel. The other half were looking at the law office from where Marshal Parsons came hurrying out.

'So your excuse for killing Siegfried is that he'd knowingly given sanctuary to a criminal and then kept his stolen money?'

'Sure, but why does that matter?'

'I was just encouraging you to get your story straight. Marshal Parsons is coming and he'll want an explanation.'

Brewster got to his feet and turned to the door.

'In that case I'd better get out of here before he arrives.' Brewster gestured to Dean. 'If you want to stay and explain what happened, do it.'

'You're going nowhere,' Dean said, taking a long step forward to intercept him.

Brewster looked at him calmly.

'Move aside or I'll tell Parsons about how you formed a partnership with an outlaw,' he said.

51

'We've never been partners and I can explain myself.'

Brewster smirked. 'In that case, feel free to head downstairs and tell your story to the marshal.'

He chuckled, and when he gestured to Dean to leave the room first Dean realized with a groan why this situation didn't cause him any concern.

'You double-crossing varmint,' he growled, stepping up to him with a fist raised.

Brewster thrust up an arm in a warding-off gesture, but he was too slow and Dean caught his cheek with a blow that knocked him aside. Brewster's feet got caught up in the blanket that had fallen off the bed and he went down all his length.

He twisted round and attempted to get up, but Dean was already on him. He grabbed his shoulder and pulled him to his feet, but only to walk him backwards until he slammed into the wall.

'You double-crossed me first,' Brewster whined. 'I know Wolfe didn't have no bounty on his head, but you still claimed I could have half. So you gave me no choice but to get my hands on some money the only way I could.'

'That's a lie. You planned all along to claim this money while framing me. You stayed out of town while I asked questions about the man who used this room. So the marshal is likely to conclude that I was the one who killed Siegfried rather than a man nobody has seen around town.'

Brewster cocked an ear, drawing Dean's attention to the rising sound of a commotion downstairs as the towns-folk started to explore the hotel.

'In that case we'd better leave before the marshal finds the body.'

Dean drew Brewster forward only to slam him back against the wall once again.

'We're not doing that. You're staying and facing the consequences, and I'll just have to hope Marshal Parsons is a reasonable man who can see through what you tried to do.'

'It'd be better for you if you didn't try.' Brewster met his eye. 'Before I shot Siegfried, he told me something interesting about Wolfe.'

Dean gulped. 'And what was it?'

Brewster noted Dean's eagerness with a smirk and then glanced at the door. People were now coming up the stairs and unless he and Dean left now, they would struggle to find a way out of the hotel unseen.

'I know what happened to Emily.'

Brewster raised an eyebrow and with a snarl Dean pushed him on towards the door.

5

Footfalls were sounding, coming to the top of the stairs. Brewster peered into the corridor. He glanced that way, then set off in the opposite direction.

Dean reckoned that that direction gave them their best chance of escape and he followed him. He was even more confident when they reached the end of the corridor and saw that there was a second set of stairs.

Brewster wasted no time in hurrying down them, but Dean dallied to listen. Marshal Parsons was being cautious, exploring the upstairs rooms slowly so, his hopes growing that they would be able to sneak away unseen, Dean hurried downstairs.

The stairs led down to Siegfried's back room, but people were milling around in the reception area, so Dean and Brewster made for a window at the back of the room. As they clambered out they heard cries of anguish going up; Siegfried's body had been discovered.

Brewster had left his horse in the shadows at the side of the hotel and he hastened to mount up, but Dean had tethered his mount at the front of the hotel. So he motioned to Brewster to ride out of town calmly while he walked round to the front. There he mingled among the gathering of people who were bustling forward to see what had happened.

As the word was spreading that Siegfried had been shot nobody paid Dean any attention. So, acting as nonchalantly as he could, he mounted up and moved away at a walking pace.

He reached the next building without problems, but then Brewster rode out on to the main drag two buildings away from the hotel.

Brewster looked at the crowd with alarm, then turned his horse away. He broke into a gallop and within moments someone shouted out that the killer was getting away.

Others took up the cry and when Dean looked over his shoulder he realized that most of the people were looking at him. So, reckoning that the situation was about to turn bad quickly, he galloped after Brewster.

As Dean reached the edge of town Marshal Parsons hurried out on to the main drag and started issuing orders. Then people scurried for their horses.

Brewster waited for Dean to catch up with him. Then, riding together, they hightailed it away into the night.

The next few hours were tense, but Brewster was adept at throwing off the marshal's pursuit. They rode fast, making sudden changes of directions to confound their pursuers in the low moonlight.

When the moon set the light level dropped, so they settled down near the summit of a ridge, from where they could keep watch in all directions. All was quiet and after an hour of watching without seeing or hearing anything untoward, Dean reckoned they had been successful.

Dean didn't reckon that Brewster would relinquish his bargaining chip by telling him what he'd learnt about Emily, so he tried a simple question.

'Where are we heading next?' he asked.

'East, partner,' Brewster replied with a sly smile.

Dean sighed. 'We're not partners.'

'You sound like a man who doesn't believe what I told you.'

'That's because you've given me few reasons to believe anything you've ever told me and plenty of reasons to reckon you'll just lead me into a heap more trouble.'

'Then start trusting me. Siegfried told me about Wolfe and about where he left Emily.' Brewster waited until Dean nodded in encouragement, then rubbed his jaw. 'So I reckon we should ride together until we get there. Then we part company.'

Dean hunched forward, trying to dampen his burgeoning hopes and concentrate on the fact that he was with a man who had tried to set him up to take the blame for Siegfried's murder back in Hawkeye.

'Until Harwood talked to me I'd never found any proof that Wolfe hadn't just killed Emily and Clement fifteen years ago,' he said. 'If Wolfe left her somewhere before he went to Hawkeye, that's even more encouraging news. So I'm not lying to you when I say that if you can lead me to a place where she once was, I will let you leave.'

'I can do better than that. Siegfried reckoned she was still there.'

Dean gulped and took deep breaths to still his racing heart.

'Then we have a deal. You show me to her, and I'll forget about your Wanted poster, the man you killed and the money you stole in Hawkeye, and anything else you may have done.'

'I'm obliged.' Brewster leaned towards him. 'But we don't have to part company. I reckon we make a good team and we can — '

'Don't push your luck.'

Brewster raised his hands and with that they returned to silence.

After another hour of watching and listening they accepted that they'd thrown off the marshal's pursuit, so they slept for a few hours.

The next day they set off at first light, heading east. Dean didn't question Brewster, preferring to take him at his word for now while watching him carefully.

He resolved that at the first sign of deception he would bring the situation to a head, but Brewster rode with apparent confidence and when they settled down that night he surprised him by revealing more.

'We should reach Nirvana by noon tomorrow,' he said. 'Then you and I will go our separate ways.'

'As we agreed, I'll need more than that. We part company when you lead me to her.'

'And that's what I'll do.'

'I've been through Nirvana several times and Emily's not there.'

'Nirvana is a big place and, as she's alive, that means she doesn't want to see you again. Perhaps she went into hiding when you were there before, and perhaps, like Wolfe, she's living a very different life under a different name.'

'Siegfried sure told you plenty while you were trying to find out what happened to Wolfe's money.'

'It didn't take long. All I got was a name and I remembered the place.' Brewster bit his lip and looked aside, as if this last comment had revealed more than he'd intended. His apparent discomfort made Dean accept that he was attempting to keep his word, that he wasn't just stringing him along until he saw a chance to flee.

Accordingly, that night he slept soundly.

In the morning, as they rode on to Nirvana, he let himself wonder what Emily had been doing for the last fifteen years and what her reaction would be when she saw him again.

Those thoughts rapidly turned dark, making the old anger that had sustained him through the first few years resurface. He rode on clutching the reins tightly and not paying attention to the journey, and it was with some surprise that he registered that Brewster was talking to him.

He shook his head and noted that they were approaching Nirvana.

'You take the lead,' he said, hazarding a guess as to what Brewster had said.

Brewster smiled, suggesting he had guessed right, and they rode on into town. Dean took calming breaths and this let him decide that, as he'd considered all the bad ways the next few hours could go, he would keep his temper so that he could find out everything he needed to know.

Brewster rode on into the centre of town and they drew up outside the Pink Lady saloon.

'This is what's going to happen,'

Brewster said. 'We're going into this saloon. We'll sit by the door and I'll tell you what Siegfried told me. Then I'll leave you to take it from there. You won't try to stop me and you won't come after me.'

'If what you've got to tell me is as useful as you hope it is, I'll honour my side of the bargain.'

Brewster didn't appear concerned by Dean's provisional agreement. Without comment he dismounted and led him inside. While Brewster collected two whiskeys from the bar Dean picked a table beside a window, from where he could see along the main drag.

'Have you ever been in this saloon before?' Brewster asked as he sat down.

Dean glanced around, surveying an establishment that was cleaner and more opulently appointed than most of the saloons he had frequented.

Two sweeping staircases on either side of the saloon room led upstairs while large double doors led through to an empty room with a stage. Only a few customers were standing at the bar in the huge saloon room, but the numerous clean tables along with the gaming tables at the back suggested this place came alive only at night.

'I usually visit the low-down places where I can gather information rather than the respectable saloons. So if I came to this establishment, it was only briefly.'

Brewster sipped his whiskey. 'Actually, the veneer of respectability is only skin deep. This is the centre for everything that's wrong in Nirvana. When Verne Allen rode with Sebastian Crow, we came here because it was safe, as did the other outlaws who frequented the Pink Lady saloon.'

'Then perhaps I erred and I should have persevered in seeking information here.'

'You didn't err. Nobody here will talk about nothing. That's why it's safe for the likes of Sebastian to come and go as they please.'

Dean took a gulp of his whiskey and

slammed the glass down on the table.

'If you're trying to angle this conversation round to us forming a partnership to go after Sebastian, you're wasting your breath. I'm not interested in nothing other than Emily's whereabouts.'

'I've accepted that. I was just helping you by telling you about this place and how you should tread carefully.'

Dean fingered his glass. 'I'm obliged for the lesson, but I'm not interested in what goes in the Pink Lady saloon.'

'You should be.' Brewster leaned over the table and lowered his voice. 'Because, you see, Emily *is* the Pink Lady.'

6

'What in tarnation are you talking about?' Dean spluttered.

Dean's outburst made Brewster glance around, but nobody was sitting at the tables near to them and the men at the bar didn't look their way.

'That's the information Siegfried gave me. Apparently, Wolfe Lord helped make the Pink Lady a success until she tired of him, and so he moved on to Hawkeye.'

'I can believe you might have found out what Wolfe did before he holed up in Hawkeye, but that doesn't mean Emily owns the Pink Lady saloon.'

'Except you've told me some things about Emily and I've seen the woman who runs this saloon. I reckon they're the same person.' Brewster tapped the side of his nose. 'I have a knack of sniffing these things out and my nose is telling me that I'm right.'

'The only knack you have is seeking out trouble.' Dean knocked back his drink. 'You'll get plenty from me if you're wrong.'

Brewster didn't meet Dean's eye as he finished his whiskey. Then he headed to the bar.

While Brewster was being served Dean again looked around the saloon room. This time he noted several paintings and logos on the walls that depicted a woman dressed in pink. He peered at the nearest representation, but it wasn't detailed enough for him to work out whether it depicted Emily.

When Brewster returned he was smiling. He placed their glasses on the table and leaned back in his chair.

'I don't reckon I'm wrong,' he said. 'I'll enjoy my drink and then I'll move on.'

'What makes you think that . . . ?' Dean trailed off when he saw what had made Brewster relax.

The Pink Lady had arrived.

A woman was now standing behind the bar and, as befitted her name, all her clothing was pink. She had her back to Dean and was in conversation with the bartender.

From the corner of his eye Dean could see that Brewster was looking at him eagerly, but he bored his own gaze into the lady's back as he tried to work out if his quest ended here.

'Well?' Brewster said after a while.

His question made Dean shake off his intense examination. He hunched over his drink and then brought the glass to his lips. His hand shook, causing whiskey to dribble over the table, so he lowered the glass back on to the table.

'It looks like her from behind, I guess,' he said, but then she turned to chat with the customers at the bar and he lowered his head.

'I warned you that this isn't a place to act suspiciously and you're going the right way about drawing attention to yourself,' growled Brewster.

Dean sighed and raised his head to smile at his companion while using the moment to look past him towards the bar. For several moments he peered at the woman, then he picked up his glass again.

Brewster picked up his own glass, regarding Dean with a raised eyebrow. This time Dean's hand didn't shake and he sipped his whiskey without trouble.

'You can go,' Dean said.

Despite his confident demeanour since leaving Hawkeye, Brewster still whistled under his breath.

'So it is her?'

'I don't know for sure yet, but it looks like Emily and even if it isn't her, I'll accept you've been honest with me and fulfilled your side of the bargain.'

Brewster nodded and knocked back his whiskey.

'In that case, remember what I said about this place. Be careful and don't do anything stupid.'

Brewster waited until Dean returned

a nod, then he headed to the door. Dean leaned back to look through the window and watch him walk away until he entered the next saloon along the main drag.

For several seconds he considered Brewster's parting advice. Then he downed his whiskey and made for the bar.

The bartender was serving in the middle of the bar, so Dean stood before him. Then, when he had a whiskey in his hand, he leaned on the bar and glanced at the Pink Lady.

She was at the end of the bar chatting with two customers. She had adopted a confident pose with a hand on a hip, and she was quick to smile as she played the part of a good hostess while the customers grinned and enjoyed her company.

Seen from the side, her nose was large, as Emily's had been, her hair was curly, like Emily's, and her height and build were as he remembered them. The most crucial piece of proof was her unrestrained laughter that he couldn't mistake.

With the matter decided he set his gaze forward and waited for her to be a good hostess with the other customers at the bar and so complete his quest. He had ordered a refill before she finished chatting and moved closer.

She nodded to the next group of customers and then walked by Dean while trying to catch his eye and smiling. He returned her gaze and that made her flinch and pause in her journey before she moved on.

Her reaction provided the final proof Dean needed. He raised his glass.

'You sure do serve a good brew, Pink Lady,' he called to her back.

She wavered, but everyone at the bar was watching her and so she turned back.

'The Pink Lady saloon is renowned for its good service,' she said, smiling at the customer nearest to Dean.

'I agree. I reckon this could be the

best whiskey I've had in the last fifteen years.'

She laughed, then moved closer. While still looking around, she leaned on the bar beside him.

'Go to a table and I'll join you later,' she whispered from the corner of her mouth. Then she turned to the bartender and raised her voice. 'Stand him his next drink. The Pink Lady likes a man who's free with the compliments.'

Her comment generated the expected round of vociferous enthusiasm from the customers. With everyone paying no attention to him, Dean collected his filled glass and made his way back to his table. He turned his chair so that he could apparently look out of the window while using the reflection to watch what happened in the saloon room.

She took her time in coming over. She continued chatting for a while before slipping away into a back room. When she emerged, she busied herself behind the bar. Then a burly man stalked across the saloon room and came to the table beside his.

The moment the man sat down she came out from behind the bar. Sporting a genial smile, she took a roundabout route across the room towards him, reinforcing the point that this was her domain.

'I can't keep calling you the Pink Lady,' Dean said when she was seated at the other side of the table. 'So what name do you answer to these days?'

'Everyone calls me the Pink Lady,' she said levelly.

'Everyone calls you that now,' he said with a glance at the man sitting silently at the next table.

She followed his gaze. 'As I don't know your intentions, my trusted guard Ormond is listening to everything we say. The moment you stop being civil, he'll deal with you in the way he deals with any customer who causes trouble.'

'That sounds like you reckon I might not act in a civil manner.'

She leaned back in her chair and spread her hands.

'You can't blame me for being cautious. I haven't seen you in fifteen years and then there you are standing at my bar. So who talked?'

'A few days ago Harwood Manning revealed some things and that led me here, but don't blame him. He'd fallen ill and he could even be dead by now.'

She smiled. 'You've become more resourceful.'

He returned the smile. 'And you've become more successful.'

'And so it would seem that we're both content with how things worked out.'

She moved to get up, but Dean raised a hand, his small action making Ormond at the next table tense his muscles.

'I'm not content, but I could be if you just tell me what happened fifteen years ago.'

'If I do that, I'm sure you won't like what I have to say.'

'Perhaps the man you once knew wouldn't accept it, but I'm a different man now. Fifteen years of searching and fearing the worst will do that to a man.'

She looked aside, appearing genuinely surprised by his response.

'If it took you fifteen years to find me, you couldn't have looked hard. I've been living here openly for most of that time.'

He shrugged. 'I guess I didn't spend all that time looking for you, but I did search until I'd used up every lead. Since then I've taken every opportunity to seek out clues about what happened to you.'

'You shouldn't have bothered. I left you with every clue you needed.'

He leaned forward to peer at her over the table.

'All you did was just disappear one day. You left no clues.'

'I did. I spent every spare moment with Wolfe Lord because I didn't want to waste my life waiting for you to come back from yet another bounty hunt.' She looked him over and sighed. 'Then I left with him because that man, for all his faults, promised me a life that sounded better than being married to a man who was never there.'

Dean smiled, finding that the truth didn't hurt as much as she seemed to think it would.

'I had hoped that would be the reason. It was a better option than you being dead.'

She pointed a stern finger at him, making Ormond edge forward on his seat.

'Don't try to make me feel sorry for you. I had a good time with Wolfe and it lasted longer than the brief interludes we had together. With his money and my hard work we built this place up from nothing.'

'So where's Wolfe now?' Dean asked, figuring that the question might reduce the chances of him being connected to the events in Hawkeye.

'He outstayed his welcome.'

'Who took his place?'

She frowned and then stood up to look down at him with her hands on her hips.

'The Pink Lady doesn't need a man at her side, and now that you've enjoyed your free drink, you will leave.'

'I can't do that. There's still one question left for you to answer.'

'You've had everything you'll ever get out of me.'

Dean fixed her with his firm gaze hoping she'd speak without prompting, but as she didn't respond he stood up and came out from behind the table.

He took a pace towards the door, making it seem that he was prepared to leave, then he swung round to face her.

'Tell me about Clement,' he said.

'Go!' Her order made Ormond stand up and roll his shoulders.

'I can't. I don't care about you and the life you've made for yourself here, but it wasn't just you who left me. You took my son away and I need to know what became of him.'

She met his gaze, gnawing at her bottom lip, suggesting she was searching for the words to explain, but then she gave a slight shake of her head and glanced at Ormond.

Dean was about to demand that she tell him, but the words remained unsaid when Ormond stormed over to him. With practised skill the big man grabbed his shoulder, swung him round, and marched him to the door with his arm held up his back.

Dean tried to keep his footing, but he was half-pushed, half-carried through the batwings and across the boardwalk. Then Ormond unceremoniously threw him on to the hardpan.

Dean rolled twice before coming to a halt on his back. He got up on his feet and turned to hurry back to the saloon, but Ormond set his feet wide apart in the doorway and directed a warning shake of his head at him.

For long moments the two men stared at each other. Then Dean bent to rescue his hat and turned away.

With as much dignity as he could muster he walked on to the next saloon. He didn't look back.

Brewster had gone into this saloon and Dean paused for a moment to consider whether he wanted to seek out a different one. Then, with a sigh, he headed inside.

7

'I can't believe that after everything you've said you'd want to drink with me,' Brewster said as he filled Dean's glass.

'You're a double-crossing varmint who tried to frame me back in Hawkeye,' Dean answered. He leaned back against the bar and cradled his drink so that he could peer down into it. 'But right now that's the nearest I have to a . . . a person I can a drink with. So I'd welcome your opinion.'

Brewster shrugged. 'I guess that at least you got an answer and that's better than not knowing.'

'I got one answer, but that's just led on to an even bigger question.'

'It is odd that she'd tell you about her life but not about your son.'

'It is, and I reckon the reason is down to her being ashamed about her life. I saw no sign of Clement, so perhaps he didn't approve of her behaviour and he did to her what she did to me and hightailed it away.'

Brewster swirled his drink and frowned.

'That's hard to accept. She's probably the most successful woman I've ever come across, so there's no reason for her to be ashamed about her life, or for you to be either.'

'A man like you wouldn't understand, but I know her, or at least I knew the woman she once was, and running a saloon that's frequented by outlaws must have forced her to make some unwelcome compromises.'

Brewster nodded. 'I don't agree, but that's not my point. She's still your wife and so now you're a success without you ever having to do nothing to build up the Pink Lady saloon.'

'I won't reveal the truth that I'm her husband so that I can claim ownership of her domain. I don't want anything from her except for the one thing she refused to tell me.'

Brewster leaned closer and winked. 'Except she doesn't know that.'

Dean shook his head. 'I'm not delivering no threats. I save them for getting people like you to help me.'

Brewster sighed. 'In that case I'll ask around. If there's a truth to be found about the Pink Lady, I'll sniff it out.'

Dean snorted. He was about to pour scorn on Brewster's boast, but their conversation had interested the man who was standing closest to them at the bar.

'What's your problem with the Pink Lady?' he asked.

Dean turned to him and offered a placid smile.

'We're new in town and were trying to work out how a woman came to be running such a place.'

'You must be new to town if you don't know that,' the man said, his easy tone suggesting he'd heard only the end of their conversation. 'She owes everything to Sebastian Crow.'

Dean flinched, then cast the man a surprised look.

'That outlaw has a huge bounty on his head. I'm surprised he'd dare to openly help her.'

'Sebastian hasn't been seen in Nirvana for a while. He takes what he needs from afar.'

'Needs?' Dean asked.

The man winced and glanced around nervously as if he'd already said too much. Then he edged away, but Brewster nodded and drew Dean closer.

'I reckon he was telling you that she pays Sebastian a cut of her profits,' Brewster said. 'In return she gets to run a trouble-free establishment.'

Dean looked at the man for confirmation and he gave a quick nod before he struck up a conversation with another customer standing near by.

'If she pays money to Sebastian for protection I can see why she was evasive,' Dean said, leaning towards Brewster. He rubbed his jaw and then lowered his voice. 'And I'd guess she's kept Clement a secret for fear of what Sebastian might do.'

'You could be right. Living in fear of what Sebastian might do to her saloon if she don't pay up is one thing, but fearing what he might do to her son is another thing entirely.'

Dean nodded. 'Which leads on to the question of what I should do about it.'

'It sure does.'

Dean waited for Brewster to say more. When he stayed silent, he nudged him and offered a prompt.

'Ever since I caught Verne Allen you've been trying to persuade me to go after Sebastian Crow. Now that I have a reason to do just that, you're suggesting nothing.'

Brewster frowned. 'I may have overstated my ability to get close to Sebastian. Verne only rode with him for a short time and I was only one of several men with Verne.'

'That's as maybe, but you know more about Sebastian than I do and some of the people you associated with could still be in town. Seek them out.'

Brewster swirled his drink. 'Are you promising me a partnership if I do that?'

'Hell will freeze over before we become partners, but you can have the bounty on him. I reckon if I free Emily from Sebastian's clutches she'll be grateful enough to tell me about Clement, and that's all the bounty I want.'

Brewster jutted his jaw, his eyes wide as he presumably weighed up the risks now that Dean had agreed to go along with his suggestion. But he didn't reply; instead he looked across the saloon room.

When Dean followed his gaze he couldn't help but wince.

Ormond had come into the saloon with two equally burly men flanking him. They spoke with a customer who pointed at the bar before scurrying away.

Ormond came towards them. He'd

covered only a few paces when the man who had spoken to them shifted even further away, while the other customers parted to leave clear space around Dean and Brewster.

'The Pink Lady warned you,' Ormond said when he stomped to a halt in front of Dean. 'It seems you didn't listen to her warning.'

'I've stayed away from the Pink Lady saloon, as I was told to do,' Dean said.

'Except you've stayed as close to her saloon as you could, and I hear you've been asking questions about the Pink Lady. She doesn't like that.'

Ormond's comments had been directed only at Dean, suggesting that even if he'd learnt with alarming speed that Dean had been talking about the Pink Lady, he didn't know that he and Brewster had arrived in town together.

It became clear when his men joined him that Ormond supposed Brewster to be just another customer who had answered Dean's questions. All three men glared only at Dean.

With a deft movement Brewster turned his back on Dean and leaned over the bar. Bearing in mind the size of the three men facing him Dean didn't reckon Brewster's help would achieve anything other than to get him a beating, too.

Dean distanced himself further from Brewster by tipping his hat to Ormond and setting off for the door. He managed two paces before Ormond stepped to the side and blocked his path.

'I've understood the warning,' Dean said. 'I'm leaving.'

'You're not,' Ormond said and then jerked forward.

Dean had seen how fast Ormond moved in the Pink Lady saloon, so he rocked back on his heels, evading Ormond's lunge, then ducked under his arm. He set off again for the door.

He figured that avoiding a fight was his best option, but that hope died when rapid footfalls sounded behind him. Then Ormond's men ploughed into his back.

The men shoved him on for several paces until he lost his footing and went down on his knees. They hoisted him back up on his feet and hurled him across the saloon room. He went spinning into a table, upending it, shattering numerous glasses and sending one of the four men seated there crashing to the floor.

Dean shook himself and then extricated himself from the debris, but when he tried to right the table the three seated men got up and surrounded him.

'Those men threw me over here,' Dean said, offering a friendly smile, but the men glared at him with meaningful grins that showed they wouldn't make the mistake of blaming Ormond and his men for their spilt drinks.

'Any man who's set against the Pink Lady has no friends in Nirvana,' one of the men said, and slapped firm hands on Dean's shoulders.

Then another man moved in, aiming to grab his arms from behind. Dean shook off the first man and turned to deliver a back-handed swipe to the second man's cheek, which knocked him over.

The third man moved in and aimed a flailing blow at his head, but Dean ducked under it. Then, with his head down, he barged into this opponent and kept moving until he lifted the man's feet off the floor.

He braced himself and tossed his opponent over his back. The man landed with a groan behind him. Dean then attempted to walk to the door again but, despite his success so far, several more men stood up from their tables to confront him.

He shoved the first man aside, punched the second man low in the chest, making him fold over, and then aimed a punch at the next man.

Unfortunately he didn't get to deliver the blow, as the forces aligned against him organized themselves and several men moved in on him.

Punches and kicks slammed into him from all directions. He squirmed from side to side as he fought to gain his freedom, but all he could see around him was a mass of angry faces and fists.

For a minute he reckoned he got in a punch for every four blows he received. Then the wall of men around him grew too dense for him to make any impact and he had to fight just to stay standing.

He reckoned if he fell over he might never get back up again. So he thrust his head down and with shoulders and hips he tried to break through the circle of men. To his surprise, when he knocked two men aside clear space opened up before him.

During the tussling he had lost all sense of direction, so now he turned on his heel until he faced the door. It was ten paces ahead and, even better, only one man blocked his route.

With no thoughts of trying to make a dignified exit he scurried towards the door. When he reached the man he tried to slip around him, but the man raised an imperious hand.

Dean snarled and made to aim a punch at the man's face, but even as he was drawing back his fist he registered that he was facing Rex Millington, the town marshal of Nirvana. At the last moment he checked his intended blow and skidded to a halt.

'You're not going nowhere until I find out what's been happening,' Millington said.

'I gather I'm not welcome here, so I was just leaving,' Dean said, settling for a politic answer.

Millington shrugged and looked over Dean's shoulder at Ormond.

'Why isn't he welcome here?' he asked.

'He's trouble,' Ormond said simply.

Millington nodded and then smiled at Dean.

'Men who make trouble in Nirvana spend a night in my cells,' he said. 'Then they leave town.'

It was approaching noon when Marshal Millington let Dean out of his cell.

The previous night Dean had given the lawman the alias he often used: Dave Carter, so as not to risk his being connected with Emily. He had been the marshal's only prisoner.

Bearing in mind Nirvana's reputation as a place that saw its share of trouble, Dean had reached his own conclusions as to where the lawman's priorities lay. So he didn't object when Millington gave him a stiff warning about what would happen if he saw him in town after noon.

He hurried outside and since time was pressing he made for the stable where Brewster had taken their horses yesterday, before they'd settled down to drink away the afternoon. When he got there Brewster was leaning against the stable wall. He smiled when he saw Dean.

'We need to leave quickly,' he said as

Dean joined him.

'I know,' Dean said. 'Marshal Millington gave me until noon to leave Nirvana.'

'There's a more pressing reason. Marshal Parsons from Hawkeye rode into town an hour ago. He's working his way along the main drag and it won't be long before he hears about two men arriving in town yesterday and getting into trouble.'

With a wince Dean acknowledged that this development was bad. In short order they collected their horses and galloped away.

Brewster had a destination in mind, so Dean didn't quiz him about his intentions until they were five miles out of town and Brewster stopped at a high point where they looked down upon a winding gully going northwards. Brewster directed him to look at two distant horsemen who were riding away from them.

'We'll be following them,' he said.

'Why?' Dean asked.

'Because I did what you asked me to do and sought out people who once associated with Sebastian Crow. I recognized those two men, Kerry and Eugene.'

'That would be after you turned your back on me and let me face Ormond and the rest of the saloon folk alone.'

Brewster shrugged. 'It would. I didn't see no point in going up against that mob, as then I wouldn't have been able to do no seeking out.'

Dean conceded Brewster's point with a rueful smile. He turned his gaze to the riders.

'So why are Kerry and Eugene worth following?'

'Because I saw them leave the Pink Lady saloon, and I gather that they ride north and then back to Nirvana on a regular basis.'

'So you reckon they relay messages to Sebastian?'

'Either that or they deliver Sebastian's cut of the Pink Lady's profits; but whatever they're doing, I reckon those men will lead us to him.'

Dean nodded and turned his horse to face up the gully.

'So it would seem that we're now going after Sebastian Crow, after all,' he said.

8

For two days Dean and Brewster followed the two riders north.

They kept far enough back to avoid detection, but whenever they caught sight of Kerry and Eugene in the distance the two men were riding along openly. They displayed no signs that they feared they were being followed or that they were riding towards the secret hideout of a notorious outlaw.

Dean had spent many years embarking on long pursuits that led nowhere more often than they led him to his quarry, and he had no trouble keeping his misgivings to himself. Brewster appeared pensive, presumably as he'd now used up his sources of information, leaving him to rely on his wits to complete their difficult mission.

Both men peered frequently at the terrain beyond the riders, but apart from noting that they were heading towards higher ground they saw no indication of where their ultimate destination might be.

On the third day of their journey they set off as usual at a slow pace, to ensure they didn't get too close to their quarry. After only a few minutes they realized that something was amiss.

The men weren't visible at all.

The previous night Kerry and Eugene had made camp on a flat stretch of ground. There had been an uninterrupted view over the terrain for several miles beyond their campsite, but now their figures were nowhere to be seen.

Dean and Brewster stopped and looked around. Then they turned to look at each other.

'It was always likely that they knew they were being followed,' Dean said. 'Perhaps they lulled us into a false sense of security and then made off in the night.'

'You're the expert at tracking men,'

Brewster said, peering around cautiously. 'I'll let you take the lead in figuring this one out.'

Dean nodded and pointed ahead to the men's camp.

'In that case, we go down there and see if we can pick up their tracks.'

'I agree, but I'm still worried this could be a trap.'

'You're the expert in being sneaky. I'll let *you* take the lead in dealing with that.'

Brewster laughed and both men rode on slowly. As they approached the camp Brewster caught Dean's eye and drew to a halt, leaving Dean to ride on alone.

When Dean reached the camp he glanced back and observed that Brewster had already dismounted and gone to ground in the low-lying scrub. Dean jumped down from his horse and fingered the ashes of the campfire.

They were warm, but that didn't prove that the men had stayed here until the fire had burnt out. He moved on, assuming a casual air, to see what else he could discover.

He found tracks leading away; they led in the same direction as the riders had been going yesterday. So, feeling that his first assumption might be correct, he looked for Brewster. At that moment he saw movement in the scrub to his right.

It was on the side of the camp opposite to the position where he'd last seen Brewster and Dean doubted that he could have covered that much distance so quickly. So he turned to the route that the tracks took and moved forward slowly, as if he were working out where the men had gone.

He watched the scrub from the corner of his eye and when he again saw movement to his right he bent over to scoop up a handful of dirt. He poked the loose dirt around to give the impression he reckoned he might learn something from it, before moving on with his head lowered.

Again he bent over to collect dirt.

Then he nodded to himself and knelt down.

He judged that he was low enough to avoid being seen by whoever was lurking in the scrub, but he dropped down on to his chest. Then he snaked along the ground, aiming for a spot about ten yards to the left of the place where he'd last seen movement.

Rustling sounded close by as, presumably, the watcher detected what he was doing. Then someone murmured a seemingly urgent alert.

Shuffling noises sounded, as of someone fast-crawling along the ground away from Dean. Dean risked raising his head.

When he'd raised himself up on to his haunches he looked in the direction of the sound and saw the top of a hat moving away from him. A second, darker form flitted through the scrub, heading towards the first man. Dean, reckoning he'd now worked out where Kerry and Eugene were, set off in pursuit, running crouched over.

He covered a dozen paces, quickly

closing the gap on the man who was crawling away, but then the second man moved through an area where the scrub was thinner. Dean now saw that this man was Brewster.

Dean's quarry must have been able to see Brewster clearly, too, as he stopped and raised himself. His arm jerked up to aim a gun at Brewster. Without hesitation Dean drew and fired his own weapon quickly, but the urgency of his need to take action meant that the lead flew wild.

The man scrambled round on the spot to look at Dean, but he made the mistake of not immediately ducking low, giving Dean enough time to aim more carefully. He fired and this time his shot caught the man in the forehead, downing him.

As Dean dropped to his knees Brewster whooped with delight and hurried over to the fallen man.

'You got Kerry,' he called. 'But I've got no idea where Eugene is, so stay down over there.'

Dean muttered to himself in irritation as Brewster ran the risk of giving Eugene more information than he needed to, but then it dawned on him that his partner was being sneaky, so he raised his voice.

'I reckon the other one's long gone,' he called. 'So I'll head back to the camp.'

'Good idea, but I'll still scout around before I join you.'

Dean feared that Brewster had destroyed their credibility by making too many distracting comments, but a few moments later Brewster's ruse had the desired effect when Eugene bobbed up from his hiding-place a dozen yards behind Brewster.

Eugene splayed rapid gunfire into the scrub in an arc that Dean reckoned stood a good chance of hitting Brewster, but Brewster had already moved on. Five yards away from the place where the last shot landed he jerked up into view, and with his first shot he blasted lead into Eugene's stomach.

Eugene staggered back for a pace, giving Dean enough time to sight him and fire a second shot into his chest that made him tip over backwards.

Brewster hurried on and briefly disappeared from view before raising himself to nod at Dean. Both men then returned to the camp where they set about following the tracks to find out where the men had left their horses.

It didn't take them long to come across them in a hollow. When they opened up a saddlebag Brewster's theory was confirmed. Inside was around $500 in gold and bills.

'So you were right,' Dean said as Brewster, smiling, riffled through the bag. 'They were delivering a cut of Emily's profits to Sebastian.'

'They were doing more than just that,' Brewster said. 'My other guess was right, too.'

Brewster withdrew an envelope from the saddlebag and held it up for Dean to take. A wax seal was on the back and the front displayed Sebastian's initials written in an ornate, looping style that Dean recognized as being Emily's handwriting.

'So she's given Sebastian a message,' Dean said as he put the envelope back in the bag.

'Aren't you going to read it?' Brewster said. 'It might contain something we can use against Sebastian.'

Dean shook his head. 'We can't complete our plan to follow Kerry and Eugene to Sebastian's hideout now, so I guess we've got no choice but to deliver the letter to Sebastian ourselves.'

'You mean we ride up to him and act all friendly like? Then, when he's accepted us, we deliver justice?'

'Sure.' Dean winked. 'After all, you're the expert in earning the trust of outlaws before double-crossing them.'

Brewster looked at the bag of money and rubbed his jaw; then he nodded. The decision having been made, the two men returned to the bodies.

They didn't know how far they would have to travel before they reached Sebastian's hideout, so to limit the chances of anyone happening across the bodies they buried them and shooed the horses away.

Then they hurried back to their own horses and resumed their journey northwards.

With no clues to follow beyond the fact that Kerry and Eugene had been riding along a straight route, both men were pensive.

★　★　★

Throughout the morning they tracked towards higher ground while keeping their eyes on the route ahead.

They stopped for a break around noon and shook their heads in dismay as they surveyed the unforgiving terrain around them.

'We could ride for days, never knowing whether we'd passed Sebastian's hideout,' Brewster said, 'or if we were still getting closer to it.'

'So perhaps we need to stop just

riding on the course Kerry and Eugene were taking and scout around,' suggested Dean.

Brewster shook his head. 'We're now planning to ride into Sebastian's hideout posing as innocent messengers sent by the Pink Lady, so if we give the impression we don't know what we're looking for, we'll look suspicious.'

'We will,' Dean said with a smile. 'But then, our cover story will be that we took over the task from Kerry and Eugene and we're only following directions.'

Brewster nodded. 'So it might not look odd that we've become lost. Even more to the point, Sebastian will want the money and the message, so if we can't find him, he'll sure want to find us.'

With that hopeful thought encouraging them they moved on, but this time they rode without trying to disguise their lack of confidence about where they were going. They tracked from side to side looking for likely places where

Sebastian could be holed up, while always moving north.

Sundown was approaching and pessimism about their chances of success was growing again when, for the first time, Dean saw a hopeful sign: a light flashed on the ridge to their right.

He didn't point this out to Brewster in case he had been mistaken, but a minute later another flash came, further along the ridge. Dean was about to ride closer to Brewster to point it out when a rapid series of flashes came that made Brewster turn to look at them.

'I reckon we've got someone's attention,' Dean said.

'We have,' Brewster agreed. 'Let's hope they get the impression from up there that we're friendly.'

Dean nodded. Brewster reached back to the saddle-bag containing the money. He raised it high and turned his horse to face the ridge before he moved on.

Dean hurried to ride alongside him and they continued at a walking pace. Dean didn't see any more flashes, but when they were twenty yards from the base of the ridge a strident voice sounded ahead.

'No further,' a man shouted.

Both men came to a halt. Brewster edged his horse forward to take the lead and raised a hand.

'We've taken over from my old friends Kerry and Eugene,' he called. 'I'm Brewster and this here is Dave.'

'Nobody said nothing about that happening,' a second man said.

This time Dean was able to work out that they were being hailed from behind a boulder around thirty yards to their right along the base of the ridge.

'They got into trouble, so they had to leave town quickly.' Brewster slapped a thigh in apparent irritation. 'You know what they're like, and if you know me from the time I rode with Verne Allen you'll know I always get the unwelcome jobs.'

'I know the kind of trouble they were always getting themselves into,' the second man said with a snort of laughter.

'And I remember Verne,' the other man said.

Murmuring sounded behind the boulder. Then the two men moved into clear view.

Both men were armed, but they kept their guns held down, suggesting they weren't the only men watching the new arrivals from the ridge. They moved ten yards closer, then stopped to look Brewster and Dean over. They turned to each other.

A brief exchange of views followed. Then the man on the right gestured for them to follow as they moved off towards the boulder.

Dean breathed a sigh of relief and brought his horse to draw level with Brewster as they rode, but Brewster didn't move on. Dean stopped and turned to him.

'Come on,' he said quietly. 'It seems that Brewster and Dave have been accepted.'

'I guess,' Brewster said, directing a worried look at him.

'You reckon this is about to turn bad?'

'I don't reckon so. I could hear some of what the two men said to each other and they seemed to believe our story.'

'So what's the problem?'

'It's not what they said, but who they are.' Brewster frowned meaningfully, giving a hint of what he was about to reveal before he said it. 'The man on the left is called Yancy and the man on the right is called Clement.'

Dean winced and looked at the man on the right. This man had his back turned and was walking away, but Dean judged him to be a young man of around twenty.

Dean groaned. 'So it seems that after fifteen years of searching I might have found my son at last, and he's a member of Sebastian Crow's outlaw gang.'

9

'Quit staring at him,' Brewster said.

'It's hard not to,' Dean replied. They followed Clement and Yancy up the side of the ridge. 'I might just have ended my quest.'

'If I were you I'd worry more about how we can stay alive for long enough to complete our mission.'

Finding that a man who could be his son was part of the outlaw gang they'd planned to destroy, Dean was no longer sure that he wanted to carry out the mission, but he kept that thought to himself. Instead, he tried to avoid looking too intently at Clement as they headed towards Sebastian's hide-out.

So far Clement had shown no sign that he recognized Dean. But then he had been only a child the last time they'd been together.

When they crested the ridge it

became clear why Sebastian had evaded capture for so long.

The steep slopes on either side of the ridge ensured that anyone approaching could be seen from some distance away, while a gash in the rock scarred the summit of the ridge. This gash was accessible only from one end and, as they skirted along the top of the ridge, Dean could see that a group of men had settled at the far end.

When they rode down into the gash, several of these men moved forward to intercept them.

'These men have taken over from Kerry and Eugene,' Clement called. Hearing this the men nodded and drew alongside to escort them to the rest of the group.

Dean had seen Sebastian Crow's likeness only on a Wanted poster, and the man sitting in the centre of the group resembled him. As Brewster was carrying the bag containing the money, he let him take the lead and, confirming Dean's guess, he approached the man in the middle.

'I don't like surprises,' Sebastian said, eyeing Brewster with suspicion.

Brewster held out the saddlebag. 'Then this will put your mind at rest. I gather you were expecting it.'

Sebastian looked Brewster over and then shifted his gaze to appraise Dean. When both men returned his gaze levelly, he directed Yancy to take the bag and bring it to him.

The sight of the money inside made him smile, but when he found the letter he nodded to each of them in apparent acceptance of their story. Then he raised the letter so that everyone could see it and tossed the bag to one side.

The other men moved in on the money to count it out while Sebastian walked on for a few paces. Then, with a glance around, presumably to check that nobody else was close enough to see the contents, he opened the letter.

It took him only a moment to read the slip of paper inside. Then he stuffed the letter in a pocket and returned to watch over the men, but he kept only half an eye on them; looking aside several times he appeared distracted.

When the men had counted the money he joined the guards. He dismissed Yancy, who headed back to the top of the ridge to resume his duties, but he told Clement to stay.

'Good news?' Clement said.

'It's the message I've been waiting for.' Sebastian smiled. 'You'll be pleased. It'll be your big chance to prove yourself.'

Sebastian withdrew the letter and let Clement read it. Clement nodded and then considered the envelope.

'My mother certainly wrote it,' he said in a low tone. He handed the letter back.

The final confirmation of his theory made Dean draw in his breath sharply. Then, feeling faint, he stumbled sideways a pace.

Seeing his reaction Brewster kicked his ankle and glared at him. Sebastian and Clement however were facing each other and they didn't display any sign that they'd noticed his apparent shock.

'Do you have any reason to doubt the message?' Sebastian asked.

'If it'd been delivered by the usual messengers rather than two men I've never seen before, I'd be happier.'

Sebastian grunted, suggesting that this aspect concerned him also. He turned to face Dean and Brewster. Dean had now regained his composure and he stood impassively while Brewster took a pace forward.

'What's the problem?' he said. 'We got given a saddle-bag to bring to you and we've done that.'

Sebastian gestured at him with the envelope.

'For the last month I've waited for this message from the Pink Lady. It details the time and place that a substantial railroad payroll will pass close to Nirvana. I intend to claim it.'

'I didn't know that, so we can't tell you nothing more about this payroll other than whatever's written down there.'

'I wasn't asking you to. What's concerning me and my young friend is whether we can trust the word of two men who nobody here has ever seen before, especially when the message is so important.'

'I told Yancy before he let us come up here that you'd met me before when I rode with Verne Allen,' Brewster said.

Sebastian narrowed his eyes and then shook his head.

'I don't remember you,' he said. He looked at Dean.

'Dave here helped me out when I saw some trouble with Verne,' Brewster said before Dean could find an appropriate response.

'That would be when Verne got shot up in a raid?'

'How do you know about that?'

'Because the sole surviving member of Verne's gang joined me last week, yet now it seems that another member of that gang has survived and turned up here.'

'Jacques is here?' Brewster tipped back his hat in a convincing appearance of surprise.

'At least that part of the story is consistent.'

'When we got raided I escaped, and now it seems he did, too.' Brewster pointed at Dean. 'Dave's an old friend and he let me hole up with him until whoever was after us moved on.'

'Jacques is scouting around with Gillespie, but they'll be back by sundown. I'll find out then whether he'll back up your story.'

Brewster agreed to that course of action with an eager nod, but Clement shook his head and stepped forward to join Sebastian.

'Even if Jacques vouches for them, this situation still feels wrong. We've got enough time before the raid for me to head back to Nirvana, check out the details, and rejoin you.'

'We do have enough time, but you're

not going nowhere. From now on nobody else joins us and nobody else leaves us.'

Clement kicked at the ground, jutting his jaw and looking as if he were searching for another way to argue his point before he accepted Sebastian's order by backing away a pace. Sebastian then gestured to Brewster and Dean to walk with him to the end of the depression.

Brewster took the lead. He picked a spot on a boulder at the side where he could sit and see everyone while ensuring that nobody could slip behind him.

Dean joined him and after the intense discussion of the last few minutes, everyone settled down to while away a sleepy afternoon.

For an hour Dean and Brewster stayed silent, by which time several men were dozing and the rest weren't paying them any attention. So Dean leaned back against the rockface behind him and drew his hat down to shield his eyes.

Brewster adopted the same posture and, the outlaws all being at least a dozen yards away, Dean whispered to Brewster from the corner of his mouth.

'What now?' he said.

'We pick our moment,' Brewster replied.

'We haven't got long.' Dean raised his hat to glance at the sun. 'Jacques and Gillespie will be back in a few hours.'

'I don't know for sure that Jacques will cause us any problems. He ran the moment you started shooting, so I doubt he saw you and it's likely he didn't see enough to work out that I was helping you.'

Dean rubbed his jaw and nodded. 'The longer we have to figure these people out and pick our moment, the better our chances will be, so we'll wait until Jacques returns.'

'What's to figure out about them other than that there's two of us and at least ten of them?' asked Brewster.

'It looks to me like there's two factions here.' Dean nodded across the depression at Sebastian and the men sitting with him and then at some other men who had congregated further away.

Brewster nodded. 'You could be right. I reckon some of these men have always been with Sebastian while others have joined him only recently.'

'In which case we need to look for tensions or divisions or lingering resentments that might be useful to us when the bullets start flying.'

'I agree, but I can't help noticing that Clement is staying close to Sebastian.'

'I was aware of that,' Dean muttered. 'So if things go badly when Jacques returns and we have to take these men on straight away, you make sure you kill Sebastian and I'll make sure I kill Clement.'

Brewster directed a horrified look at him, so to avoid discussing the matter Dean got up and walked away.

10

'We've got trouble,' Sebastian said, raising his voice and alerting everyone to the fact that someone was heading down into the depression. 'Only Gillespie has come back.'

Sundown was still an hour away and, as Jacques hadn't returned with Gillespie, Dean joined the others who were moving over to meet him.

Since Dean had stated his intention of killing Clement he'd avoided Brewster and tried to strike up conversations with the other men to help him figure out who might represent the biggest dangers here.

He hadn't spoken to Clement yet, and he wasn't sure whether he wanted to do that.

'First thing this morning we came across some trouble,' Gillespie said when he reached the bottom of the depression. 'We heard distant gunfire, but we couldn't find the source. So I'm reporting back while Jacques stayed behind to check it out.'

'You did the right thing.' Sebastian turned to Dean. 'Did you hear any gunfire this morning while you were on your way here?'

'No,' Dean said. 'Then again, we weren't listening out for any.'

'Gillespie and Jacques were patrolling between here and Nirvana, so you were all travelling through the same area.'

Dean shrugged. 'We didn't see them and it sounds like they didn't see us. So either they weren't doing their job properly or we weren't in the same area.'

Gillespie bristled at the accusation, but Sebastian accepted his explanation with a frown. Then everyone returned to their previous relaxed positions.

Brewster directed an approving nod at Dean and came towards him. Fearing that he might want to talk to him about his decision to kill Clement,

Dean stayed with the rest of the group, engaging in casual chatter.

Before long he had spoken at least briefly to everyone other than Clement. Then he settled down in his previous position at the side of the depression.

Later, food was passed round, after which Sebastian allocated guard duties through the night. He ignored Dean and Brewster so, with the onset of night Dean dozed.

With the morning came animated activity. Overnight Sebastian had decided to move on to the location of the planned raid. Apparently it was a two-day journey and the raid would happen on the third day.

Despite his previous order that nobody would leave the group, Sebastian dispatched two men on an unspecified mission. Then he directed Gillespie to join Jacques and inform him that they should meet up with the main group later when they were satisfied about the reason for the gunfire.

If they were to find the reason, it would almost certainly be because they had come across the aftermath of the gunfight with Kerry and Eugene. Dean wasn't unduly worried about that, as the potential problem of meeting Jacques had been postponed again.

He was less happy to see that Clement was the only man with whom Sebastian discussed his plans, giving the impression that he was the most trusted member of the group.

When they moved out they rode west for an hour before they veered away towards Nirvana. Dean rode beside Brewster, and when they rested up in late morning he didn't avoid being alone with him as he had done since yesterday.

'I've accepted that you don't want to talk about Clement,' Brewster said when they were sitting down and the rest of the men were talking amongst themselves. 'But you'll always regret taking a decisive action that you can't undo.'

Dean shrugged and glanced around to check nobody was paying them any undue attention.

'I helped to create this problem, so I have to be the one who solves it.'

'But you've spent the last fifteen years looking for him.'

'I've spent those years looking for outlaws, and he's an outlaw.'

Brewster shook his head. 'You've pursued men like Sebastian Crow, but other men can be given a second chance.'

Dean snorted his disbelief, but then he noticed that Brewster was beaming proudly.

'If you're putting yourself forward as an example of what happens when you get a second chance, you're not making a good case,' he jibed.

'Perhaps, but maybe before you make a decision you can't reverse you should talk with Clement and find out whether he's more like Sebastian or more like me.'

'Both choices are as bad as ... '

Dean trailed off, then conceded Brewster's point with a smile.

While they were resting he made no move to carry out Brewster's suggestion, preferring to wait for a moment when his and Clement's paths crossed naturally.

As it turned out an opportunity didn't arise that day or in the evening, neither was he presented with a situation in which they could converse through the long day of riding that followed.

Late in that second day Sebastian directed them along a trail that wound its way around the steep side of a pass. At a point where they were a hundred feet from the ground and the trail spread out to provide a wide flat area, he stopped in front of a cave, where he stood back while directing everyone to look inside.

Everyone dismounted and moved forward, and some of the men exclaimed in surprise when they saw that the two men he'd sent off on a mission before they'd left the hideout had arrived here first.

These men had brought a wagon, which they'd hidden in the cave along with enough supplies to feed everyone for several weeks. Dean noted that the men he'd assumed were part of Sebastian's inner circle hadn't looked surprised.

Sebastian reported that they had now reached their destination. They would hole up here for the raid that would take place the next day.

He directed his men to drag the wagon out of the cave on to the flat area so that they could unload it. Then they needed to take up positions along the pass and settle in for a long wait until the payroll passed by below.

Clement happened to be standing near to Dean and Brewster, and as Sebastian hadn't given them duties Brewster looked at Clement.

'What do you want us to do?' he asked.

'Just keep out of the way,' Clement

said. He pointed at the cave. 'So stay in there where we can keep an eye on you.'

'It sounds like you still don't trust us.'

'I don't, but if you keep your heads down and give us no trouble tomorrow, you can leave after the raid.' Clement chuckled. 'But make sure you move fast, or whoever survives the gunfight might think you're behind it.'

Brewster muttered to himself and moved away towards the cave leaving Dean standing beside Clement. This situation presented him with a natural opening to a conversation for the first time. Dean sighed, which made Clement turn to him.

'Does your mother know you're involved with this?' Dean asked.

Clement stared at him in surprise. Dean couldn't blame him. He'd spent the last fifteen years fearing that his son was dead, so he'd rarely thought about what he would say if he ever got a chance to talk to him again.

Since finding out that Clement had gone bad, he'd spent the last two days thinking up and then rejecting various versions of what he ought to say. Even so, his first comment was one he hadn't considered making.

'What's that to you?' Clement muttered with a sneer.

'From what I know of the Pink Lady, I'm surprised she told Sebastian Crow about this payroll delivery, and I'm even more surprised to find out that her son will be riding with the raiders.'

Clement moved closer and looked him up and down with disapproval.

'I've never seen you before, so you can't know her that well, and you must have known what you were delivering to Sebastian.'

'I assumed the saddlebag contained money to pay off Sebastian, so it makes no sense that her son is benefiting from that pay-off.'

Clement's eyes flashed with anger but then, with an amused grunt, he appeared to dismiss the matter.

'My mother always has this effect on men. They invariably take her side and that's why I have to make my own way. My cut from this raid will let me set up on my own.'

'In other words you've decided to take the easy way, no matter that it's the wrong way and no matter that men will probably get killed tomorrow.'

Clement set his hands on his hips and glared at Dean in open-mouthed shock.

They were a few dozen yards from the nearest man, so nobody would know what they were talking about, but it would be obvious that they were having a disagreement. That being so, on seeing Clement's reaction Brewster emerged from the cave while the men who had dragged the wagon out of the cave stopped sorting through the supplies and turned to watch them.

'Nobody can speak to me like that,' Clement muttered, stabbing a finger against Dean's chest, 'and especially not some no-hope messenger boy who's been sniffing around my mother.'

Dean batted Clement's hand away and then as his anger grew, he shoved Clement's shoulder.

'Perhaps if someone had spoken to you earlier you might not be setting out to ruin your life now.'

Clement righted himself and stepped forward to confront Dean, but rapid footfalls sounded and Sebastian joined them. Sebastian wrapped his arms around Clement's chest from behind and dragged him back a pace.

'I don't know what this is about, but I'll have no fighting in the camp,' he said in Clement's ear. 'Save it for tomorrow and for the right people.'

'He was saying some mighty odd things about my mother,' Clement said, struggling.

When Clement failed to dislodge Sebastian Dean moved closer.

'I didn't say nothing bad about the Pink Lady,' he said. 'You're just awful touchy about something.'

He would have said more, but then

Brewster reached him. Brewster grabbed his shoulder and told him firmly to come with him in to the cave.

'Your friend's got the right idea,' Sebastian said while Clement squirmed as he tried and failed to dislodge Sebastian's grasp. 'You two will leave whatever problem you have with each other until after the raid. Then you're free to sort this out.'

His comment made Clement stop struggling, then he nodded. Sebastian waited for a moment, then he released Clement, who took a pace away and pointed at Dean.

'Until later,' he said.

'Until later,' Dean said. Then he let Brewster lead him away.

'At least you two are talking now,' Brewster said when they reached the cave.

Dean snarled and shook Brewster's hand away.

'Don't try to make light of what just happened. I've spoken with him at last and I was right. Clement is a good-for-nothing varmint and he has just removed every doubt I ever had about what I have to do to him.'

Brewster raised an eyebrow. 'So you did have doubts?'

'Of course I did, but no longer.'

'If I were you, I'd listen to those doubts.' Brewster lowered his voice to a whisper even though they were the only men who were now in the cave. 'Try to bring him to justice by all means, but make sure you don't kill him.'

'I may have no choice. He won't hesitate to kill me.'

'Then that's even more of a reason to stay your hand. Perhaps you can live with killing your son, but no matter what you think of him, I doubt he'll be able to live with killing his father.'

Dean shook his head. 'Emily will never tell him the truth about who I am, so he won't find that out and besides . . . '

Dean trailed off as voices were raised outside. Both men stood still, looking towards the cave entrance, until Sebastian called out and clarified what was happening.

'It's Jacques,' Brewster said with a grimace. 'He's arrived.'

11

'If Jacques has a problem with us, make sure you take out the men closest to Sebastian first,' Dean said as he and Brewster walked to the cave entrance.

'I'm not convinced these men will start shooting at each other when all hell breaks loose,' Brewster said. He shrugged. 'But I don't have a better plan.'

At the cave entrance they stopped. There they could watch Jacques and Gillespie ride nearer. Sebastian stood in front of the wagon watching them, while several of his men, including Clement, swung round to watch Dean and Brewster as they awaited Jacques's pronouncement on whether they could be trusted.

'Report,' Sebastian said when Jacques and Gillespie drew up.

'We tracked down the source of the

gunfire,' Jacques said. 'It is bad news, but I don't reckon it should give us any problems. Kerry and Eugene must have been coming out to see us when they got shot up.'

Sebastian swung round to point at the cave.

'Except the message from the Pink Lady still got through, and it was to come here.'

Brewster and Dean tensed. Jacques peered in to the cave and pointed at Brewster.

'What's Brewster Kelly doing here?' he demanded, his voice rising in anger. 'He's the one who lured Verne into a trap and got him killed.'

Jacques then swung his finger round to point at Dean, suggesting that he'd worked out that he'd been involved, too. But he didn't get to accuse him; Brewster drew his gun and fired at him. His shot flew wild, but Brewster broke into a run and blasted a second shot that hit Jacques high on the chest, downing him.

Brewster hurried to the far side of the wagon. Dean reckoned he was doing the right thing, as if they stayed in the cave they could get pinned down and then picked off, so he thrust his head down and sprinted after Brewster.

Sebastian's men stared at Brewster and then at Jacques's body. Their wide-eyed expressions displayed their shock at the sudden turn of events. It was plain that they didn't know how to react to what appeared to be the end to a long-festering dispute.

Sebastian was the first to get his wits about him. He pointed at Brewster.

'They're trying to double-cross us,' he roared. 'Gun them down.'

Brewster dived for safety as Sebastian's men drew their guns. Dean was several paces behind him, and as most of the men levelled guns on him he hurled up his arms and dived forward.

Gunshots tore out and lead peppered the dirt behind him. He hit the ground, rolled over a shoulder and scrambled to safety beside Brewster, who was already peering over the wagon at the forces aligned against them.

'If we get out of this alive, we'll sure earn our bounty,' Brewster said. Dean had raised himself and was standing hunched over beside him.

'Just keep your wits about you and we'll be fine,' Dean said.

'It's us two against more than a dozen and I don't see no sign of anyone making a move to help us.'

'Then it's time to recruit people to our side.' Dean raised his voice. 'Hey, Sebastian, you should never have let new men join you, but now it's time to end this. Everyone that's with us, do it now like we agreed.'

Brewster directed an approving nod at him. Then they waited.

Rapid footfalls sounded on the other side of the wagon as Sebastian's men took up positions facing them.

Every second that passed increased the possibility that Dean's assumption that there was distrust within the group was wrong and his ruse had failed.

Dean was preparing to shout a second taunt in the hope of spreading consternation when a gunshot ripped out, followed by a rapid volley of shots.

None of the firing hit the wagon, but frantic cries went up on the other side of the wagon.

'It worked,' Brewster said, slapping the side of the wagon in approval.

'I never doubted it for a moment,' Dean said with a smile.

Then he edged along to the back of the wagon. When he peered around the corner he saw that one man was lying on his back with his chest holed while most of the men were scurrying towards protected positions on either side of the cave.

Dean hurried them on their way with four rapid shots. The last shot caught one man in his side before he reached the safety of a boulder beside the cave. He toppled over and then lay still.

Dean edged further away from the wagon, but he failed to see where the rest of the men had gone to ground, and he scurried back out of sight. While he reloaded Brewster fired over the top of the wagon, ducked down.

'It's chaos out there,' Brewster said happily. 'I can't work out who's firing at who or even where most of the shooting is coming from.'

'As long as they're not firing at us I don't care,' Dean said.

Brewster nodded. 'And all we'll have to do next is take on whoever survives.'

Brewster raised himself again. His gaze rested on something that was happening beyond the cave; he furrowed his brow and turned his head as if he was watching a running man.

'Is that Sebastian?' Dean asked.

Brewster shook his head and ducked down as a thud sounded on the other side of the wagon, as of someone running quickly to reach a safe position. Dean continued to look at Brewster, but when Brewster failed to meet his eye he realized why Brewster wasn't telling him who had moved to the other side of the wagon.

He hurried back to the corner and edged out with the intention of firing at the men outside the cave, but then he found that Clement was slipping around the back of the wagon towards him. The moment Clement saw him he snapped up his gun arm, but with only a moment to react Dean slapped his arm aside, slamming it against the wagon.

He pushed forward and pinned Clement back against the tailboard. That position put Dean in full view of the men by the cave, but he put that from his mind as he dashed Clement's arm against the wagon, forcing him to drop his gun.

A gunshot kicked splinters out of the wood a foot from his right arm, so he grabbed Clement's shoulder and shoved him along to the corner. Another shot tore into the wood behind him as he followed Clement slipping into cover.

When he saw Dean's captive Brewster smiled and raised himself to fire, but this time gunfire ripped along the top of the wagon, forcing him to duck down before he could pick a target. Brewster directed a warning glance at Dean a moment before hoofbeats thundered towards the back of the wagon.

Dean pushed Clement along and forced him down on to his knees. Then he swirled round to face the onslaught, but when the riders came into view their gazes were set on the trail ahead, and they galloped past the wagon.

Sebastian was in their midst. Dean took aim at him, but just then another man rode past the wagon, blocking his view. This man was looking down at him, drawing back on his reins. Dean raised his gun, but before he could fire a volley of gunshots tore across the man's back. He cried out and slumped forward.

His spooked horse reared up and swung towards the wagon. The mount came down heavily against the tailboard, making the wagon roll forward until the man fell off the horse.

The horse then went skittering on after the others. Looking back at the wagon, Sebastian saw the man's plight. He shouted to his men, who all drew to a halt. Sebastian swung round to face them.

Brewster moved to hide under the rolling wagon, but Clement put a hand on one side of it and vaulted up on to the back. Dean reckoned he had the right idea and he followed him. Brewster clambered up a moment later.

As Dean rolled over in the back of the wagon a ferocious volley of shots hammered along its side, keeping them pinned down. Then a second burst of gunfire tore out. This volley didn't hit the wagon and Dean assumed it was the men defying Sebastian who had fired.

He raised his head and looked around as he tried to make out where their allies were. To his surprise he saw movement above the cave and along the higher parts of the pass.

He didn't think the men who had been with Sebastian should have been able to gain those positions so quickly, but clearly the men up there were shooting at Sebastian, for Sebastian then swirled round in the saddle to return fire.

Then Sebastian and the three men with him stopped firing and beat a hasty retreat. Dean aimed at Sebastian's fleeing back, but the wagon lurched, ruining his aim, and the next he knew he was sliding along the base of the wagon.

With a groan he worked out that the wagon had rolled forward for several yards and now the front wheels were slipping over the edge of the flat area. With only the slope down into the bottom of the pass ahead of him, he could do nothing other than wave his arms as he sought something to grab hold of to stop himself sliding forward.

His hand hit the side of the wagon. With a twist of his wrist he grabbed a secure hold, but the wagon continued to roll and tip forward. Then it speeded up, causing Dean to lose his grip and tumble along the base until he slammed into Brewster. The collision wrenched Brewster away from his precarious hold on the side of the wagon.

Gunfire was still rattling away, but they stood no chance of being able to return fire as the wagon speeded up and headed down into the pass.

The side of the pass was steep and he doubted that the wagon could continue rolling for long. Sure enough, amidst a grinding of axles and a cracking of timbers, the wagon tipped over on to its side.

Dean was propelled out of the wagon and for several moments he had the worrying feeling of being airborne. Then he slammed down on his side and went tumbling along the narrow path.

The world appeared to turn a dozen times before he managed to stay his progress. Then he lay on his back looking up at the sky, which still seemed to be swirling around him.

Gingerly he raised his head in time to see the wagon crash down on the bottom of the pass in a mass of broken wood and dust. Then he flexed his limbs and found that he'd survived the fall intact.

He got to his feet and looked up the side of the pass.

He had tumbled around a hundred feet down from the scene of the gun battle and the sound of shooting was still tearing out. He couldn't see anyone up there so he looked about him for Brewster and Clement.

He found Brewster lying on his back some twenty paces further down the slope, while Clement was another twenty paces further on. Clement had recovered quicker than Brewster had and was pacing towards the supine man.

Clement had also grabbed a gun, presumably Brewster's, and he held the gun levelled on him as he walked.

Dean raised his own gun and set off down the slope to intercept him. In his confusion caused by the crashing wagon and the gunfire, Clement didn't show any sign that he'd seen him.

Clement had halved the distance to Brewster when he firmed his gun hand and, fearing that he was about to shoot Brewster, Dean broke into a run. He thrust his gun out, his breath coming in harsh gasps as he faced a choice between shooting Clement to save Brewster or letting Brewster be killed.

'Stop!' he shouted. Flinching, Clement swung round to find Dean bearing down on him.

Clement turned his gun away from Brewster to aim at Dean, but then Dean slammed into Clement's chest and carried him down the slope for several paces until both men tripped over. They hit the ground, Clement landing on his back and Dean falling on top of him.

In their battered state both men took long moments to recover. Then each of them tried to subdue the other.

Clement was the less effective as he

could only buck his hips weakly, while Dean settled his weight down on his son and then dashed the gun from Clement's hand.

'Get off me,' Clement muttered.

'I'm not letting you shoot him,' Dean said, raising his gun up into Clement's line of sight.

Clement considered the gun and then stopped struggling.

'You've just made the biggest mistake of your life,' he said with surprising confidence. 'Any man who threatens a lawman is looking for more trouble than he can handle.'

Dean blinked hard and then jerked back in surprise.

'Lawman?' he said.

12

Clement glared up at Dean until Dean moved the gun away from him, then he nodded.

'I'm Deputy Clement Kennedy,' he said. 'I'm Marshal Millington's deputy.'

'That's hard to believe,' Dean said, shaking his head. 'Sebastian trusts you, and Millington's so ineffectual he must be in the pay of the outlaws who infest Nirvana.'

'Millington only wants people to think he's being ineffectual and nobody knows that he secretly recruited me. Clearly it's worked, as outlaws like you believe I was one of you.'

Dean rubbed his forehead, and that helped him to accept that he hadn't been so shaken by his tumble down the slope that he'd misunderstood what Clement was saying. Trying to suppress the smile that threatened to break out, he rolled off Clement and held out a hand to help him to his feet.

'I'm no outlaw. You're not the only one who isn't who he claims to be.'

Clement regarded him cautiously, then took the hand.

'And who are you?'

Brewster coughed. Dean looked up the slope and saw that Brewster had raised himself on to an elbow and was glaring at him.

Getting his meaning, Dean nodded, accepting that telling Clement the full truth about his identity in the middle of a gun battle could be nearly as big a mistake as the one he'd almost committed a few moments ago.

'I'm a bounty hunter. I've been trying to bring Sebastian Crow to justice.'

'You mean that you aim to deliver justice for money,' Clement said with a sneer. He released Dean's hand and stood up unaided.

'Sure, but then again that is the point of a bounty being put on a man's head.'

Clement snorted. 'The kind of men

who are interested in bounty are no better than the men they capture.'

'I've heard that view before and I'd be prepared to discuss it with you, but right now a gun battle is still raging up there amongst Sebastian Crow's men. We need to work together to take on whoever's left standing.'

'And that's the kind of mistake that men who only care about money make when they get involved in a matter that should be left to lawmen.' Clement gestured up the slope. 'Sebastian's men aren't fighting amongst themselves. Marshal Millington ambushed them.'

Dean narrowed his eyes as he thought back, then he grimaced.

'That explains why I thought the shooting was coming from higher up the pass than his men could have reached. So you've been relaying information back to Millington about where Sebastian will be.'

'So now you're starting to understand. It's pity you've only figured out some of it after Sebastian's hightailed it away from here.'

'And what part haven't I understood?'

Clement shook his head and turned to go back up the slope, but Dean grabbed his arm, halting him. Clement glared down at the hand, but Dean didn't remove it, so Clement looked up to face him.

'It's taken six months to set up this trap and my mother risked her life to make it happen. When Sebastian demanded money for protection she let him think he'd won by turning the Pink Lady saloon into a safe haven for outlaws, except she fed information to Millington. This raid was supposed to pay Sebastian off; it should have been the last raid he'd ever make.'

'Because Millington knew about it?'

Clement shook his head. 'No, because there never was no payroll for Sebastian to raid in the first place. A whole heap of lawmen is going to be heading along the pass tomorrow. With Millington above, them below, and me in the middle Sebastian wouldn't have stood a chance.'

Clement glared hard at Dean until he saw comprehension dawn in Dean's eyes. With a gulp Dean removed his hand from Clement's arm.

'Except we started shooting a day before you could spring the trap,' said Dean, 'and with all the plans about to collapse Millington had no choice but to start the assault early.'

'Sure, and now you've ruined months of planning and let Sebastian escape.' Clement said angrily. 'But I guess a man like you will only be annoyed that you won't get your hands on a bounty.'

Dean reckoned anything he said would only anger Clement even more, so he raised his hands and backed away. Clement looked him over with contempt, then turned again to make his way back up the slope.

Dean went to join Brewster. He helped him to his feet, then both men watched Clement walk away.

'That went well, then,' Brewster said levelly.

'How in tarnation have you come to that conclusion?' Dean murmured.

'Turns out Clement isn't an outlaw like Sebastian or even like me, and that has to be better than all the other things that have been going on in your mind for the last two days.'

Dean shook his head, unwilling to let Brewster's optimistic take on the situation cheer him.

The shooting was now only sporadic, but Clement walked cautiously with his head bowed. Dean followed, figuring that helping finish the task he'd inadvertently come close to foiling was his best course of action.

As Clement approached the cave he walked towards the spot where the wagon had gone over the cliff. Dean didn't care to join Clement in his cautious inspection and he hurried past so that he could be the first to explain the situation.

Clement glared at him and waved at

him to stay back, but Dean ignored him and kept going. First, he saw Millington's men clambering down the side of the pass, then when the cave came into view he saw that the gun battle was all but over.

Only one of Sebastian's men was still on his feet. He was running past the cave entrance towards a stray horse until several lawmen fired together, cutting him down. The moment the man hit the ground those men swung their guns round to aim at Dean. In a shocked moment Dean realized that they wouldn't know he was coming to help them.

He raised his hands high and stopped. At least four men still aimed at him; two other men were looking past him.

Dean glanced over his shoulder and saw that Brewster had thrust his hands high but was keeping his head lowered to disguise his identity. Clement called out to the men.

'Don't worry about them,' he shouted.

'They *are* the men who started the shooting, but they're not with Sebastian. They're bounty hunters.'

Several groans sounded, but nobody spoke until Marshal Millington came into sight. He walked on until he reached the edge of the slope, from where he looked down at Dean. His upper lip curled in a sneer.

'You're the man I kicked out of a cell a few days ago,' he said. 'Back then you never said you were a bounty hunter.'

'Back in Nirvana I was trying to find out information about Sebastian Crow,' Dean told him. 'I asked the wrong people too many questions and found myself on the wrong side of a beating.'

'Then some things never change for you. You've just ruined a plan that took — '

'Your deputy has already explained it to me, but I wasn't to know,' Dean snapped; everyone showing contempt for his actions was beginning to make his blood race. 'As far as I was concerned I was risking my life taking on Sebastian and a whole heap of outlaws.'

'And now we'll have to risk our lives again carrying out a mission we would never have had to attempt if I hadn't let you out of jail.'

Dean took a step up the slope, meaning to remonstrate with Millington some more. Then the thought hit him that prolonging this argument ran the risk of the marshal coming down the slope and talking to him and Brewster.

If Millington were to recognize Brewster, his presence would be hard to explain. So Dean pointed along the pass.

'Then you'd better go after Sebastian. The more time you spend arguing with me, the longer it'll take you to capture him.'

Millington gazed at him scornfully. His fellow lawmen moved forward to flank Dean, but the marshal limited himself to only pointing at him.

'Forget about collecting the bounty

on Sebastian Crow's head and stay out of my way. If I ever see you in my town again I'll find a reason to throw you in a cell, and this time I won't let you out.'

Then he turned away and gathered his men around him to discuss tactics. It took them only a few moments to agree about the route Sebastian had taken, after which Millington's men started climbing up to the top of the pass, presumably to collect their horses and chase the outlaw.

Millington waited for Clement, who hurried over to join him. Dean decided he wouldn't risk speaking to his son again, but Clement, as he passed by, stopped and looked at Dean with contempt.

'Take care of yourself, son,' Dean said with a thin smile. 'Sebastian could still be a lot of trouble.'

Clement didn't appear to notice Dean's fatherly adjunct to his request; his only reaction was to raise a finger and point at him. Then, shaking his head, he appeared to decide not to make his planned retort and he hurried on.

The marshal patted Clement on the back and smiled at him with approval. Then he ushered him on to precede him in leaving the pass.

Dean watched the two men clamber up past the cave. He couldn't help but compare the respectful way Clement looked at the marshal with the contempt he'd shown for him.

Presently Brewster joined him and the two men stood silently until the lawmen had moved out of sight. Then Dean sat on a rock and held his head in his hands.

'Your son is a mighty fine young man,' Brewster said, sitting down beside him. 'And I'm sure he'll be safe. Millington's men outnumber Sebastian's and — '

'Quit trying to find a good side to this. Emily left me fifteen years ago because she decided a man who chased after bounty wouldn't make a good husband or a good father, and she was right. The moment I meet them again, I ruin her scheme and I put Clement's life in danger. They'd both be better off if I'd never found them.'

'That's true, but there's nothing you can do about that now.' Brewster slapped his back and stood up to look along the pass. 'All you can do is make things right from now on, and that means we have to find Sebastian first.'

Dean looked up. 'And so get our hands on the bounty, I assume?'

Brewster spread his hands. 'We are bounty hunters, after all.'

'I'm a bounty hunter. You're just some outlaw who had useful information that could help me, except none of it has helped.'

Dean lowered his head again to contemplate his hands, leaving Brewster to murmur to himself, presumably as he sought a way to get him to start thinking positively. Then, with a grunt of irritation Brewster walked on up the slope.

Dean heard him moving around, but

he felt too weary to care about what he was doing.

When he'd embarked on his quest fifteen years ago he had accepted that he might never succeed and that if he did, it was likely any answers he might find wouldn't be comforting.

Even in his darkest times he'd never considered whether if Clement was alive he would look at him with disdain, or that he would be justified in doing so.

Presently he heard the clopping of approaching hoofs. He raised his head to see that Brewster had mounted up and was leading Dean's horse.

Brewster stopped on the edge of the steep slope down into the pass and leaned forward in the saddle to speak to him.

'You can't sit there feeling sorry for yourself for ever,' Brewster said. 'It's time to go.'

Dean waved Brewster away. 'If you want to go after Sebastian, do it, but I'm not going anywhere with you.'

'I'm not going after Sebastian.'

'Then you've talked yourself into some sense, but that changes nothing.' Dean stood up and started making his way up the slope. 'We're not partners, so we have no reason to do nothing together now.'

'You don't get to ride away from me that easily, not when we have a mission to complete.'

Dean shook his head, but he stayed quiet as he climbed up to the flat stretch of ground. Then he mounted his horse and looked around at the aftermath of the gun battle.

From down the slope he hadn't noticed that Millington had left two men behind to deal with the bodies. These men had stopped what they were doing to watch as the two riders appeared. He returned their gaze until they resumed their grim task; then he turned to Brewster.

'If we're still going to ride together, you need to start talking sense. How can we complete our mission if we're not going after Sebastian?'

Brewster winked. 'Because we're going to let Sebastian come to us.'

'We delivered the message to Sebastian and you started the shooting, but I doubt he'll care enough about our role in the ambush to come looking for us.'

'I agree.' Brewster lowered his voice. 'He won't want revenge against *us*.'

Brewster gave Dean a long look until, with a gulp, Dean realized what Brewster's emphasis meant. Then he swung his horse around to head out of the pass.

13

It was approaching midnight on the second day after leaving the pass when Dean and Brewster reached the outskirts of Nirvana.

Marshal Millington had promised Dean that he'd suffer dire consequences if he saw him again, but they had taken a direct route to town and reckoned the lawman should still be elsewhere, pursuing Sebastian. However, Marshal Parsons from Hawkeye could still be here, looking for them.

They rode around the outskirts of town until they found an outlying abandoned building, where they holed up for the night.

In the morning they discussed tactics before making their cautious way into town. When they reached the main drag they stopped between two buildings and contemplated the quiet town.

The Pink Lady saloon was a hundred yards away. Even in the morning people were gravitating towards the saloon, so the two of them waited until a group of men went by, then slipped in behind them.

They chatted to each other in a casual manner, which let them reach the saloon without encountering any problems. Once inside, Dean picked an empty table in the corner.

As it was likely that Brewster might not have been noticed when he was last in there, he collected two coffees from the bar and joined Dean. The two men leaned back and with their hats drawn down low, they waited for an opportunity to speak to the Pink Lady.

She was standing at the corner of the bar, holding court with several men. None of the other customers appeared to be paying undue attention to Dean and Brewster.

'Your wife sure is a popular lady,' Brewster said. 'If Sebastian Crow figures out that he rode into a trap and returns here to accuse her of helping to set it, she'll just have to click her fingers and a hundred men will leap to her defence.'

'I reckon you're right, but if it's true about the number of outlaws who frequent this place, just as many men could be loyal to Sebastian.'

'Either way, this is a situation that could turn nasty real quick, so what's your plan?'

'It's nothing more than making sure Emily knows about the danger that she could be facing. Then we'll see about finding somewhere to lie in wait for Sebastian.'

'I'm pleased that you're being more positive. We'll need that when . . . ' Brewster trailed off and indicated that Dean should look across the saloon room.

Dean looked in that direction and winced. They had been spotted.

Ormond, the guard who had thrown him out of the saloon, was glaring across the saloon room at him. Within moments another man, who'd been with Ormond when he'd followed Dean to the nearest saloon, had joined him. They moved forward.

One man advanced to block their path to the bar while Ormond headed towards them. He took a circuitous route that ensured they couldn't make a run for the door.

'The first time, you got a warning,' Ormond said, setting himself in front of their table. 'The second time, you got a beating. Now, it gets serious.'

'I know,' Dean said levelly. 'The Pink Lady's life is in danger, so I had to risk returning. I need to speak with her. Then I'll leave you to do your job and protect her.'

'You don't get to do anything with the Pink Lady.' Ormond smiled thinly. 'But you can speak to me.'

Dean gulped down his coffee and shook his head.

'What I have to say is for her ears only.'

Ormond frowned. Dean stood up,

glancing covertly at the bar as he did so. Numerous customers were between him and Emily, so he doubted she was even aware of this confrontation.

Then Dean moved his hand swiftly to his holster and pulled out his gun. Even as the barrel cleared leather he registered that Ormond had already whipped out his own gun. With a lightning movement Ormond aimed the weapon at him, forcing Dean to stay his hand.

'Move that gun another inch and you'll be full of holes,' Ormond said.

From the corner of his eye Dean saw Ormond's associate draw his own gun and aim it at Brewster, forcing him to raise his hands above the table.

'I'm pleased to see you can draw fast,' Dean said. 'The Pink Lady will need men like you on her side soon, but as I said, I only want a brief talk with her.'

Their confrontation had now attracted the attention of the men at the surrounding tables. Customers peeled away from the potential source of trouble, causing a ripple of consternation to spread across the saloon room. Within moments the conversation at the bar had stilled and everyone there turned towards them.

Then Emily's voice broke the silence. 'I'll deal with this,' she said.

Nobody moved as she came out from behind the bar and walked across the saloon room to join Ormond.

'I have a message for you,' Dean said.

'This is a friendly saloon. The Pink Lady doesn't listen to men who have their guns drawn.'

With his eyes set on Ormond, Dean opened his hand and let his gun slip back into its holster. When Ormond reacted only with an approving grunt, he looked at Emily and tried to convey with his earnest gaze that he had important and private news to convey.

'Satisfied?' he asked, showing his empty hands.

'I will be when you've given me your message and left.'

'In that case, I've heard that Marshal

Millington launched an attack on Sebastian Crow's outlaw gang. Most of the outlaws were killed, but Sebastian escaped.'

Emily nodded, although a slight twitch in one eye showed that this revelation caused her concern.

'I'm sorry it came to that,' she said, raising her voice so that everyone could hear. 'Sebastian has been a good customer here in the past and the marshal is always welcome here. Is there any more to your message?'

'That is the message I wanted to relay to the Pink Lady saloon.'

Dean hoped she'd notice his choice of words and sure enough, she turned on the spot, sporting a smile.

'In that case I'll bring you a drink to show my gratitude. I'd advise you not to annoy Ormond in future.'

She patted Ormond's shoulder and then caught his eye with a stern look that conveyed an order, which Dean presumed meant that Ormond should ensure they left afterwards.

When Dean sat down, Ormond moved back for a few paces. As the saloon room bustle returned to normal Emily walked back to the bar and collected two glasses of whiskey.

She took her time and when she returned to Dean's table few people were looking in their direction. She sat down and pushed the glasses towards Dean and Brewster.

'Deputy Kennedy is fine,' Dean said.

She drew in her breath sharply. Then she gathered her composure by looking aloft for several moments before lowering her head to look askance at Brewster.

'Don't worry about me,' Brewster said. 'I know everything, and you need to listen to Dean.'

'What happened?' she asked, turning back to Dean.

'Brewster and me were after Sebastian Crow for the bounty. We tried to get close to him, but he got into a gunfight with the marshal. Sebastian fled with three of his men, so the marshal and his deputies followed him. We decided to return here to warn you.'

Brewster glanced at Dean and smiled, acknowledging the politic version of events he'd just provided.

'I don't need to be warned about Sebastian,' she said, although her uncertain tone suggested otherwise.

'Sebastian is no fool. He's sure to work out that he'd been lured to the pass with false information and when he goes looking for revenge, the trail of deceit will lead him to Nirvana.'

She nodded and they sat silently for a while. Dean sipped his drink as he waited for Emily to steer the conversation round to the obvious subject that neither of them wanted to discuss.

She watched his glass intently, seemingly making the point that the moment he'd finished his whiskey this meeting would end. When he put the glass down with only a puddle of whiskey left in the bottom, she leaned forward over the table.

'Don't make me ask,' she said.

172

'In that case, I talked with Clement, but I didn't tell him who I am.'

She sighed with relief. 'Thank you for that. As you've gathered, I don't want him ever knowing that you're his father.'

Dean swirled the liquid in the glass. 'He has massive contempt for bounty hunters, so I assume you did tell him something about me.'

'I told him the truth: that his father cared more about tracking down outlaws than he did for his family.'

'That was a lie and you know it.'

Emily gave him a long look before shaking her head.

'I don't want to argue with you, but in any case, a mixture of hearing about the men who deliver justice for bounty and spending time with Wolfe Lord resulted in him developing a healthy ambition to be a lawman.'

Dean couldn't help but remember Clement leaving the pass with Marshal Millington. Clement's relaxed attitude with the marshal suggested that his decision to become a deputy meant he'd picked his own father figure, but Dean didn't want to give her the opportunity to pour more scorn on him.

'So I did contribute something to the man he is today,' he said, offering a more optimistic take on the situation.

'Only by your absence.'

'Except he carries my name, so you can't have been too ashamed of — '

'He's not interested in you. He's a grown man now who knows his own mind and he won't care if some stranger turns up and claims that he once used to know me well.'

Dean downed the last of his whiskey and slammed the glass down on the table.

'That's all I ever wanted to know. Seeing what a fine man he's grown into ends my quest.'

'Which means you can leave Nirvana with a clear conscience and a clear mind, and never return.'

Dean stood up and stepped around

the table to stand beside her.

'I'll do that, but take care. I'm sure that Sebastian will come back to Nirvana. When he does, you might need more than just the protection of men like Ormond, Marshal Millington, and Deputy Kennedy to stop him.'

'The Pink Lady needs no man at her side.'

She stood up and they faced each other. Dean met her gaze, searching for some hint of the woman he once knew, but he saw only the blank eyes of someone who wanted just one thing from him: his departure.

'I'll do as you ask and don't worry.' He lowered his voice to a whisper. 'I have no interest in running a saloon, so I'll never tell anyone who I really am and I'll never claim this place for my own.'

Her eyes flashed and her hand jerked up to slap his face, but she stayed the motion, presumably only because they were in a public place. Dean then tipped his hat and moved away slowly.

He stopped beside Ormond and smiled. In response Ormond rolled his shoulders as a warning not to return. Then, when Brewster joined him, they made for the door.

'You need to learn when to shut up,' Brewster said. 'That was going well until the end.'

'I was trying to put her mind at rest,' Dean said.

'Then you failed, and you've ruined any chance of us being allowed to come back in here again.'

'Why would we want to do that?'

Brewster sighed, but he said nothing until they reached the door.

'Because while you were busy talking too much, I was watching everyone, and the man who looked most annoyed by your revelation about Millington ambushing Sebastian Crow was Ormond.'

Dean grimaced and swung round to look across the saloon room. Emily was now slipping behind the bar while Ormond was standing where they'd left him and was watching them intently.

'So you're saying the fast-draw gunslinger protecting Emily is a man who sides with Sebastian?'

'I sure am.'

Their delay in leaving made Ormond take a pace forward and Dean turned away. Then, not waiting for Brewster, he hurried outside.

He moved away from the saloon door at a brisk pace and turned round the corner of the building with the intention of going back to the derelict building that they'd made their base.

He'd taken only a few paces when a man stepped out from behind a post and blocked his path. Dean veered away, but then he recognized Marshal Parsons and came to a halt.

'I reckoned that you were still in town,' the marshal said. 'So now you've got some questions to answer.'

Dean backed away for a pace and looked to one side, meaning to tell Brewster to flee, but Brewster wasn't visible. He turned back to Parsons and smiled.

'I'm sure I can answer all your questions,' he said.

Parsons snorted with a show of disbelief and signified that Dean should walk on ahead. When they reached the main drag Brewster still wasn't in sight, but Parsons showed no sign that this concerned him.

Parsons led Dean along to the law office, which was unoccupied. Then he sat on the edge of the desk and invited Dean to explain himself.

Dean provided an abbreviated version of recent events that avoided mentioning Brewster and instead concentrated on his search for Verne and then for Wolfe and Sebastian. When he'd finished, Parsons went over the story several times before, with a sigh, he set his hands on his hips.

'So in brief, your story is that you're a bounty hunter and you went to Hawkeye to look for an outlaw called Wolfe Lord?'

'That's the truth,' Dean said.

The marshal paced back and forth

across the law office, shaking his head.

'So why did you kill Siegfried Forester, a man who didn't have a bounty on his head?'

While conducting his interrogation Parsons hadn't mentioned Brewster other than to dismiss the brief sightings of him in Hawkeye as being irrelevant.

Despite Brewster having sneaked away to leave him to face trouble alone, again, Dean reckoned that he owed a debt to Brewster for his forceful encouragement not to kill Clement, so he dismissed the thought of mentioning him.

'As I said, I didn't kill Siegfried. I just wanted to prove that the man lying up in the cemetery was Wolfe, and killing the hotel owner wouldn't have helped me to do that. In fact, the information Siegfried gave me helped me to work out where Sebastian Crow was and the lure of the bigger bounty drew me here.'

'Marshal Millington is searching for Sebastian and he's not looking in town.'

'I reckon Sebastian will be coming to Nirvana soon, and if I'm in the law office, I won't be able to do anything about that.'

'You won't be able to do anything to anyone no more.' Parsons folded his arms. 'The moment Millington returns and gives me permission to take you out of his town, we'll be heading back to Hawkeye.'

14

Their interview concluded, Marshal Parsons directed Dean to a cell in the corner. However, in deference to the fact that he was using another lawman's office, he didn't lock it.

It was a journey of at least a day from the scene of the failed raid and Dean hadn't revealed what had happened in the pass. So if the raid had taken place at the scheduled time, the lawman ought to arrive around noon.

As noon came and went and then the day wore on, Parsons looked out of the window more frequently and started to get more animated.

With nothing else to occupy his mind, Dean also couldn't avoid getting nervous, as every hour that passed increased the chances that Sebastian had got away from the lawmen.

It was just after sundown when, with

a sigh of relief, Parsons hurried to the door and threw it open. Dean couldn't see what was happening outside, but he heard men dismounting and then Parsons and Millington talking.

The discussion continued for a while. Then, when Millington came in, he looked across the law office at Dean and slapped a hand to his forehead.

'You again!' he said. Parsons smiled.

'Did you get him?' Dean asked.

'That's not your concern,' Millington snarled, his anger providing all the answers Dean needed.

'I came here because I reckon Sebastian will return to Nirvana,' Dean said, figuring that, unprompted, the lawmen wouldn't give him any time to explain himself.

'I figured that too, but if he does me and my deputies can deal with him.' Millington turned to Parsons. 'I've had enough of this varmint. You can head back to Hawkeye with him whenever you want.'

'I'm obliged,' Parsons said. 'I reckon

I've wasted enough time kicking my heels here, so I'll leave straight away.'

With that, he beckoned Dean to leave his cell so that he could cuff him. While he was dealing with Dean, Millington directed his men to come inside, where he proceeded to give them orders.

One of the men was Clement. Dean tried to avoid looking at him, but by the time Parsons led him to the door, Millington had finished his instructions. Clement turned round to watch him be led outside, his upper lip curled in a sneer.

'I'm pleased to see that this time you've annoyed another lawman so much you've been arrested,' he called after him.

'I made a mistake back at the pass,' Dean said, halting a step from the doorway.

'You made your biggest mistake when you decided to deliver justice purely for money.'

Parsons stepped up close to Dean from behind and put a hand on his shoulder to urge him on. Dean knew he should let Clement have the last word and leave, but he couldn't stop himself speaking up.

'We all do things that seem right at the time, but which might get judged badly later.'

'Perhaps, but from the look on Parsons's face, I reckon you're the one who's about to get judged.'

'He sure is,' Parsons said and pushed Dean on, but Dean dug in a heel and stopped himself in the doorway. Then he whirled round to face Clement.

'Do your duty, son, but remember that Sebastian will be looking for revenge and your mother could be the target.'

Clement's eyes flashed as he prepared to snap back a harsh retort, but Milligan nodded on hearing Dean's comment and moved forward. Dean didn't get to see what happened next as, with a determined shove, Parsons moved him out on to the boardwalk.

Then the marshal led him down the

main drag to the stable. Dean offered no further resistance as he moved on with his head bowed.

Parsons had commandeered an open wagon, which was empty apart from two large crates in the back. He directed Dean to sit opposite the crates so that he could tie his cuffs to the wagon's side.

Dean didn't struggle but just looked back at the law office. When Parsons clambered on to the seat Dean was pleased to see Clement leave the office and walk on alone towards the saloon.

As the wagon moved off he watched Clement walking away, but Clement didn't look back at him. When an outlying building took Clement and the saloon out of sight, Dean settled back against the side of the wagon.

Parsons was clearly being true to his word in being eager to return to Hawkeye. He maintained a lively speed, giving the impression that he would keep moving well into the night. After tugging at his bonds for a while, Dean accepted that he wouldn't be able to free himself.

He settled down on his back with his feet planted against the side of one of the crates. He idly kicked at the wood, and his light taps made the lid shake and then slide to one side.

The movement surprised him and he sat up straighter. He was even more surprised when Brewster peered out of the crate and looked at him with a finger pressed to his lips. Dean nodded and settled down, leaving Brewster to turn to face the front and watch Parsons.

The marshal showed no sign of knowing anything was amiss, so Brewster raised himself slowly and stepped out of the crate. Then, with his gun drawn, he edged forward until in a sudden burst of movement he came up behind Parsons.

He wrapped an arm around Parsons's neck while jabbing the gun into his back.

'Don't do anything stupid,' he said. 'I

just want your prisoner.'

'I should have listened to the people who said they thought two men were involved,' Parsons said as he drew back on the reins.

'You'd have been better occupied investigating Siegfried Forester's activities. He harboured Wolfe Lord, a known outlaw, and he associated with a man with a bounty on his head, Verne Allen. Siegfried's demise was overdue and your town will be safer without him.'

'If you've got a story to tell, return with me to Hawkeye and make a statement. Then I'll investigate this the proper way.'

'I can't do that. We're going after Sebastian Crow and we haven't got a moment to lose.'

Brewster disarmed the marshal and relieved him of the key to Dean's cuffs. Then he signified that Parsons should get down off the wagon, which he did without further complaint.

Brewster clambered into the seat and with his face averted from the marshal in an attempt to mask his identity he swung the wagon round and headed off at an angle to their previous course. He drove on for several minutes, then he glanced back. Parsons was no longer visible.

Brewster drew the wagon to a halt and jumped into the back.

'I'm obliged,' Dean said when Brewster had removed his cuffs. 'I could get used to you stepping in when I'm in trouble.'

'Then you'll soon get a chance to repay me,' Brewster said as he returned to the driver's seat. 'Before I hid in that crate, Marshal Millington rode into town and he and his deputies looked agitated. I reckon that means Sebastian is close by.'

Dean joined Brewster on the seat. 'I saw them arrive, too, and you could be right, so we need to get back to Nirvana quickly.'

'Do you still reckon we'll be able to claim Sebastian's bounty?'

'I'll be honest with you. That'll be

tough. Before I can lodge a claim I'll have to prove my innocence, but I'll face that problem when I come to it. The first thing is to stop Sebastian.'

Brewster nodded, but he still drove on along the same course for another mile to confuse the afoot lawman when he followed them. Then, after a while, he turned the wagon round to head towards Nirvana.

Dean reckoned that Parsons had travelled for around half an hour before Brewster had made his move. So, with Brewster urging as much speed as he could from the wagon's horse, they soon espied distant lights flickering in the town ahead.

When the main drag came into view there was no sign of trouble. Brewster slowed the wagon so they could approach in a calm manner that wouldn't attract attention. He steered it to the side of the stable, where they climbed down and moved along to peer around the corner of the building at the town.

They confirmed their first impression that nothing untoward was happening. Then, as the Pink Lady saloon was on the other side of the quiet law office, they made their way around the backs of the buildings to come out beside the saloon that was nearest to their destination.

There, waiting in the shadows, they watched. The main drag and the saloon at their side were quiet, but from the Pink Lady saloon came the sounds of raucous laughter and music playing.

After a short while Brewster drew Dean's attention to the only man who appeared not to be making his way towards the revelry. This man was standing on the other side of the main drag, facing away from them.

'I reckon I remember that man,' Brewster whispered, narrowing his eyes. 'He's one of Sebastian's men who got away.'

'I can't see him clearly, but you could be right,' Dean said. 'He seems to be watching something.'

'Or waiting for something to happen.'

Dean nodded. Then they waited to see who was right.

Ten minutes passed before the man set off towards the Pink Lady saloon. When he walked into a patch of stronger light Brewster grunted, indicating that he had identified the man correctly.

A moment later two other men came out of the shadows, one of them appearing from the side of the saloon, the other emerging from only a dozen yards away from Dean and Brewster. When he could see the two men clearly Dean identified them as being the couple who had escaped with Sebastian in the pass.

The three of them walked quickly, meeting up at the entrance to the Pink Lady saloon, where they conferred briefly before turning to face the door. A minute passed, then Ormond came outside.

Ormond glanced around, then shooed them through the door. The men hurried inside but Ormond stayed a moment or two to look around before he followed them inside.

'So now we know where everyone that we have to worry about is, other than Sebastian,' Dean said.

'But we know where and when all the trouble will break out, so Sebastian won't be far away.'

The two men turned to each other. Then, exchanging quick nods, they hurried on towards the saloon.

They stopped beside the first window, where Dean edged forward to peer inside.

Ormond and the three men were standing a few paces beyond the door. Apart from the four of them the saloon room was deserted; even the bar was closed, but people were crowded in the wide doorway that led into the other room.

The music was playing in that room, where many customers were craning their necks to look towards the stage and others were uttering whoops of delight; it was clear that they were enjoying the entertainment. Dean assumed from the raucous laughter and applause that it involved dancing saloon-girls, but he couldn't see the stage.

The three men were consulting with Ormond, who was gesticulating. The conclusion to the debate appeared to come when Ormond backed away while the three men moved on across the room towards the entertainment.

'We have to make our move now before it's too late,' Dean said.

Brewster glanced up and down the main drag and nodded.

'There's no sign of anyone else making a move, so Sebastian must already be in there.'

Brewster backed away from the window and rooted around on the ground until he found a discarded bottle. Then he moved on to the door, where he put his back to the wall and held the bottle high in one hand and drawn gun thrust out in the other.

Dean guessed his intention and

positioned himself on the other side of the door from Brewster. He nodded to his colleague. Brewster smashed the glass down on the ground while Dean stamped a foot and uttered a cry of alarm.

Inside the room Ormond muttered something and then came to peer out over the batwings. When he saw Dean he snarled and pushed through the doors, emerging with his gun drawn and aimed at Dean.

'You had your final warning,' Ormond said. 'Yet you just don't ever seem to listen.'

'I ignored the warning because I'm looking for Sebastian Crow,' Dean said. 'Where is he?'

The question made Ormond flinch. Brewster took advantage of his momentary confusion to step up behind him and press his gun into his back.

'Answer his question,' he snarled in Ormond's ear.

'I'm not doing nothing to help your friend,' Ormond said.

'A pity,' Brewster said. Then he fired.

The muffled blast made Ormond stand up straight before he toppled over and hit the ground. Brewster wasted no time in vaulting over his body and hurrying into the saloon.

Dean dallied to check that Ormond was breathing his last, then he followed Brewster. Sebastian's men were now standing behind the customers who filled the doorway into the other room. With the loud music playing they showed no sign that they'd heard the gunshot.

Brewster had already trained his gun on the doorway, but numerous people were standing between him and his targets, so he held his fire as he stalked across the room. Dean hurried to join him, then, side by side, they moved towards Sebastian's men.

Dean didn't reckon they'd be lucky enough to reach them without being recognized, but he hoped to get close enough to shoot without fearing that a mis-directed shot would hit a customer.

The stage was just coming into view over the customers' heads, revealing a line of high-kicking dancers, when in a coordinated move the men barged their way into the room.

A moment later a loud cheer went up along with much arm-waving that briefly hid the dancers and also let Sebastian's men disappear from view. With a snarl of irritation Dean and Brewster hurried on to reach the doorway.

When Dean raised himself to peer over everyone's heads, he couldn't pick out Sebastian's men, but from his last sighting of them he judged that they had been trying to reach the left-hand side of the stage.

On the stage the dancers bowed and waved to the audience. Then to loud cheers they bustled off through a door in the back corner. The cheering grew even louder when the dancers were replaced by a woman dressed all in pink.

Emily had arrived.

15

As calls rang out around the room requesting the Pink Lady to sing various songs, Brewster turned to Dean.

'I didn't know that she sang,' he said.

Dean shrugged. 'Neither did I. Then again, it seems that there's plenty I don't know about her.'

'Either way, we need to make sure this isn't her last song.'

Dean grunted his agreement. Then he picked out two men who looked small enough for him to barge aside easily and stepped forward.

He managed to slip between these men, but then the packed-in customers swallowed him up and he struggled to make further headway. Curses sounded to his right, presumably as Brewster made his own attempt to move forward, making a wave of men knock into Dean and then sweep him along.

Dean saw that he was being pushed in the general direction of the stage. Unfortunately, he was moving towards the side opposite to where Emily was encouraging the customers to offer suggestions for songs that she could sing by pointing at various men while holding a hand to her ear.

Even worse, he caught his first sight since entering the room of one of Sebastian's men. This man was elbowing customers aside as he fought his way towards the middle of the stage.

Those he moved aside whirled round to remonstrate with him, but they soon quietened. That let Dean work out that Sebastian's other two men were following in the wake of the first man and that they were dealing out threats.

There were still at least a dozen men between the leading man and the stage so, as he reckoned he still had enough time to catch up with the other two, he turned towards them and set off.

He didn't manage more than a few

short paces, as the men around him were packed in tightly and the bustle was still moving everyone towards the front of the stage. Dean saw that there was clear space around one side of the stage, presumably because the placing of a pillar meant that the view there was poor.

As he could reach the stage from the side he stopped fighting against the prevailing movement of the crowd and let it carry him on. He halved the distance across the room quickly, but then a clear space filled up and he stopped moving.

The disgruntled customers who had been forced into a poor position started digging in their heels and then trying to move back. Dean found himself wedged in tightly and unable to go in any direction.

He looked for Brewster. He couldn't see him, but only a few men were between Sebastian's men and the stage.

Emily had now made her choice of song; she raised a hand and turned aside to compose herself, which encouraged everyone to stop shouting suggestions. As the room became quieter Dean took a deep breath and called out.

'The Pink Lady is in trouble,' he shouted. 'Help her before she's killed!'

Unfortunately, the moment he started shouting other men joined in, mistaking his plea for the beginning of a chant.

'Pink Lady! Pink Lady!' the customers shouted and after only a few repeats the chant carried to all corners of the room, drowning out Dean's message.

Emily turned to the front with a smile on her lips and waved a hand in time with the chants, but several men who were close to Dean must have heard his demand, and they turned to him.

'Sebastian Crow and his men are in the room,' he shouted, although his voice carried only to those nearest to him. 'They aim to kill her.'

As nobody would know of the reason for Sebastian's ire, he received bemused looks. Then several men started shouting at him all at once, but as the confusion grew he encouraged it by yelling his warning again.

This had the desired effect. People fought to move away from him until, for the first time since he'd entered the room, he found himself standing with enough room to move freely.

He oriented himself to face the shortest route to the stage and saw that the first of Sebastian's men had already got there and was now urging the other two men to join him.

Dean had taken only two long paces forward when a hand slapped down on his shoulder. He turned, hoping that Brewster had arrived to help him, but to his surprise it was Clement who stood behind him.

'What did you do with Marshal Parsons?' Clement demanded.

'He's fine, but your mother won't be,' Dean said. 'Sebastian Crow is here and he means to kill her.'

Clement shook his head. 'I can

believe Sebastian wants to harm her, but Marshal Millington chased him out of town half an hour ago and I guess he's still in pursuit.'

'I hope that's the case, but Sebastian's flight could have been a distraction to lure Millington out of town. Either way,' Dean pointed to the middle of the stage, 'three of Sebastian's men are over there.'

Clement looked where Dean pointed, but with unlucky timing the customers surged forward, blocking the view so that even Dean couldn't pick out Sebastian's men.

'I'm not taking the word of a bounty hunter who ruined one lawman's raid and has now escaped from another lawman.'

Time was pressing, but Dean could see no obvious way to talk Clement round; he hunched his shoulders in resignation. However, when Clement raise his hand to direct him to the door, he pushed forward, knocking Clement backwards into the circle of men who surrounded them.

Then he set off for the stage, this time abandoning all caution and forcing his way on with fists and kicks. He barged past several customers, but then one man took exception to being pummelled and he returned a flailing blow that knocked Dean into another man, upending them both.

Dean went sprawling on the floor where he lay floundering with his limbs entangled with the fallen man. His desperation growing, he slapped the man aside, but by the time he'd got up on his haunches, Clement had fought his way to him and was standing over him, shaking his head.

'You have to listen to me,' Dean shouted over the chanting that was showing no sign of petering out. 'Your mother — '

A gunshot rang out, silencing the chanting. Clement whirled round to face the stage. With a fearful heart Dean leapt to his feet, but to his relief Emily didn't appear harmed.

She was backing away from the front of the stage, staring at the spot where Dean had last seen Sebastian's men. Even though Dean had thought the room was so tightly packed that nobody could move freely, space opened up around the area to reveal the first man to have reached the stage.

The man was standing hunched over clutching his chest, which was rapidly reddening. Brewster was standing five paces away from the wounded man with his gun drawn, darting his gaze from side to side as he looked for the other two men.

The wounded man fell forward on to his chest. Seeing this, the customers who were standing behind Brewster moved in on him.

Two men grabbed Brewster's arms from behind. Brewster struggled, but as nobody knew that he was trying to save Emily's life, other men moved in to secure him.

'This is Deputy Kennedy!' Clement shouted, now finally understanding the situation. 'Everyone get down. There are two more killers in the room.'

For several moments nobody moved, but then, in shocked reaction to Clement's words, men dropped down to their knees. The movement had yet to reach the stage when Dean again picked out Sebastian's two men.

He raised his gun to aim at the nearest man. Clement glanced at him; when he saw where Dean was aiming he levelled his own gun on that position.

The customers around the stage dropped down, leaving Sebastian's two men exposed, but also giving them a clear view of everything around them. Both men snapped up their guns to aim at Emily at the back of the stage.

Two crisp shots rang out, the reports only a rapid heartbeat apart. Thankfully Dean and Clement had fired first, aiming at different men. First one man and then the other toppled over sideways, their backs bloodied.

Even before the men had hit the floor

the surrounding customers pounced on them and pinned them down.

Clement nodded to Dean. In a now silent room they both walked towards the stage. They aimed for the spot that Dean had been trying to reach before, and now that people had moved aside they reached the side of the stage in moments.

Dean clambered up on to the stage and looked across the crowded room. He couldn't see Sebastian Crow and when Clement joined him and also peered around, he shook his head.

Dean ended his survey of the scene by looking at Emily, who had her back pressed up against the back wall. She was looking at Clement, worry furrowing her brow, showing the same concern for his safety as Clement was showing for hers.

The customers then caught on to the danger that was still ongoing and everyone started looking at the men who were standing nearest to them. So, now that the situation was becoming clear to everyone, Dean set off across the stage.

He walked towards Emily. He was the only person looking in that direction and so was able to see the door in the back corner of the stage as it swung open.

Part of the outline of a man appeared in the shadows. Dean could see only an arm, but clutched in the man's hand was a gun. It was already aimed at Emily.

Dean stopped and raised his own gun, but before he could take aim Emily saw where his aim was directed. She glanced at the door and, with a casual wave of a hand she made the same gesture she'd used to encourage applause.

A gunshot popped.

Then the man jerked away out of sight and Dean set off at a run. He registered that Emily hadn't moved since the shot, and he'd covered only three quick paces when the man came back into view. He was Sebastian Crow.

Dean aimed at him, but he stayed his fire when Sebastian dropped down to his knees, a blood-soaked hand clutching his chest. Then he keeled over to land face first on the stage.

Dean ran towards him, then halted, stopping between Emily and Sebastian. He watched Sebastian writhe and then lie still. He turned to Emily, who was now facing the front of the stage and smiling at a relieved-looking Clement.

She turned to Dean and with a twitch of her wrist she slipped the pistol in her hand back up her sleeve.

'As I told you,' she said, 'the Pink Lady needs no man at her side.'

16

'I can see that you can take care of yourself,' Dean said.

He still moved on and knelt beside Sebastian, but Emily's gunshot had hit him in the heart and he was already dead. He looked up and sought out Brewster, but the men who had been holding him had disbanded and he wasn't visible.

Concerned customers were crowding in around the stage, but further away confusion and recriminations were breaking out, suggesting that men were here who might be loyal to Sebastian.

Dean judged that plenty of other men here would support the contrary view and he could leave them to deal with the problem. Clement appeared to have reached the same conclusion when he hurried across the stage to take his mother's arm and escort her to the door behind Sebastian's body.

She didn't object, so Dean lingered, to look again for Brewster. This time he saw him slipping into the saloon room having presumably concluded that as Emily had killed Sebastian they had lost all hope of claiming a bounty on him.

Then he hurried after Emily and Clement, joining them in the room at the back of the stage from where Sebastian had sneaked up on Emily.

Emily had already gathered several of her workers around her and was giving them instructions to quell the trouble, so Dean faced Clement, who tipped back his hat and frowned, acknowledging his problem.

'Without your help this situation could have had a tragic conclusion,' he said, 'but I can't avoid the fact that you created this situation and that you're an escaped prisoner.'

'The charges against me are a misunderstanding,' Dean said with a relaxed smile, 'but whatever you decide is fine with me. All I wanted to do was put right my mistake.'

Clement sighed and set his hands on his hips.

'I guess now that this is over and no innocent parties have been harmed by your actions I can accept that your mistake wasn't that bad. You were just trying to bring down Sebastian Crow and you weren't to know that plans were already in place to do that.'

'I wasn't, and no matter how much contempt you have for me and my kind, bounty hunters can be useful to lawmen. A good deputy town marshal shouldn't hate us for what we do.'

'I know. It's not your fault that I don't like you.' Clement shifted from foot to foot and then shrugged. 'The thing is, my father was a bounty hunter and it's hard for me to be objective about it.'

Dean gulped. 'What happened to him?'

'He died when I was young, chasing after yet another bounty.'

Dean struggled to find an appropriate response. When he glanced aside he saw that Emily had finished giving orders and was looking at them with concern.

'I'm sure he was only doing what he thought was best for his family, and I reckon your father would be proud of the way you turned out.' Dean smiled. 'Perhaps one day you'll find that you can forgive him for abandoning you.'

'Perhaps I should, and maybe there's a way to do that right now.' Clement returned the smile and then pointed at a door on the other side of the room. 'I didn't see you again after what happened on the stage. So take the back exit and run.'

Dean met Clement's eyes and when Clement nodded he slapped his shoulder. Then, not trusting himself to speak, he moved past him.

Clement hurried out on to the stage to join the others who were dealing with the disturbance.

Dean glanced through the doorway. He could see that the situation already appeared to be under control, several men having been rounded up while other customers retreated to the saloon room in a calm manner. Then he turned back to find Emily was blocking his path.

'Thank you,' she said.

'Is that for trying to help you or for not telling him?'

'Both.' She took a deep breath. 'And I mean it when I say this: I hope you got what you came here for.'

'I got everything but a bounty, but I can get that anywhere and it never was the most important thing in my life.'

She nodded and then gnawed at her bottom lip before moving closer to him.

'I know you gave a false name to Millington, but with Marshal Parsons looking for you, your real name will probably get mentioned before too long. Clement's no fool. It won't take him long to think the unthinkable.'

'What'll you do then?'

'If he suspects you're alive I'll tell him the truth.' She sighed, looked him over, then lowered her head. 'And if he

213

doesn't piece it together, I'll pick my moment and tell him the truth anyhow.'

'Then I got far more here than I ever hoped to get.' Dean rubbed his jaw. 'Perhaps if I'm ever in the area again, I might call in at the Pink Lady saloon for a drink and a chat with Emily, a woman I used to know well.'

She looked up and winked. Then she moved on past him to go to the stage. She held on to the side of the door for a moment, then turned back to him.

'Decent men are always welcome in the Pink Lady saloon,' she said, 'but only if they call me the Pink Lady.'

She waited until he nodded, then she moved out on to the stage.

Dean watched the doorway, but she didn't reappear, so he hurried on to the back exit. He peered outside; nobody was visible and he scurried along the backs of the buildings to reach the stable on the edge of town.

People were milling about everywhere. He doubted whether he could reach the derelict building where he'd left his horse without being seen. He reckoned he'd have no choice but to risk it, so he moved around the corner.

To his surprise the wagon he and Brewster had arrived on was still at the side of the stable; even more surprisingly, Brewster was on it and waiting for him.

'You took your time,' Brewster said, urging him to hurry up.

'I had some things to discuss,' Dean told him when he joined him on the seat.

'By the look of your smile that discussion went well.'

'It did.'

'Good, because this situation could still end badly.' Brewster pointed to the right. 'I saw some men get sent out of town and they left afoot. So I reckon that means Marshal Millington's not far away and they went to collect him.'

Dean nodded and pointed to the left.

'Marshal Parsons should be heading to town coming from that direction and he should get here soon, too.'

Brewster raised the reins and looked ahead and behind them.

'So we have an irate lawman who hates us on one side and another irate lawman who hates us on the other side. Which way should we go?'

Dean looked back and then forward. He faced Brewster.

'I'll let you choose, partner,' he said.

We do hope that you have enjoyed reading this large print book.

Did you know that all of our titles are available for purchase?

We publish a wide range of high quality large print books including:
Romances, Mysteries, Classics
General Fiction
Non Fiction and Westerns

Special interest titles available in large print are:
The Little Oxford Dictionary
Music Book, Song Book
Hymn Book, Service Book

Also available from us courtesy of Oxford University Press:
Young Readers' Dictionary
(large print edition)
Young Readers' Thesaurus
(large print edition)

For further information or a free brochure, please contact us at:
Ulverscroft Large Print Books Ltd.,
The Green, Bradgate Road, Anstey,
Leicester, LE7 7FU, England.
Tel: (00 44) **0116 236 4325**
Fax: (00 44) **0116 234 0205**

NOLAN'S LAW

Lee Lejeune

After his mother and father die, and the girl he hopes to marry turns him down, Jude James decides to abandon his rented homestead and ride for the West along with Josh, a young exslave seeking sanctuary. Eventually they fall in with a gang led by Brod Nolan, who claims to rob the rich to feed the poor. But there is more to this than meets the eye — and the two friends find themselves embroiled in a series of bloodcurdling encounters in which they must kill or be killed . . .